insanity

by

bob tillman

What follows is a work of Fiction. Mostly. Any references to persons living or dead are intended as parody and homage and not intended to cause any harm to them personally or professionally.

BACKSTORY

This book is an attempt to fulfill a prophecy made by my 4th Grade English teacher.

"Someday Robert will be a professional writer," wrote Mrs. Ellison of the Denison (Texas) Independent School District.

It's also one of the most wonderful ideas ever to pop into my head. It's part of a fantasy that originally included the creation of a few story ideas for a popular television show. The "plan" was supposed to go something like this:

1. The popular show's showrunners read my ideas.
2. The producers then buy them.
3. I present my pitches for two new shows, which included some character crossovers built-in.

The first new show was multi-layered and would be creatively therapeutic for the showrunners (who are very talented people whom I admire), plus people would enjoy characters skipping between the two genre-diverse shows.

Who knows, maybe the second show would actually be made into a movie!

Timewise, the first new show and its characters are introduced to the public, become popular, and then the second new show starts airing.

I never heard any feedback or any response regarding my original story ideas.

Rather than give up on the two new shows, I decided to flesh out the pitches and write them as a short book. Why should I give up on my dreams?

So without further ado, let's move on to the rest of the book, telling a few tales about The Three Ladies (as I call them in my head) who work for ZBS Television and Paradox Motion Pictures Studios Project Support Department:

Jackie Faraday

Tonya Manning

and

Jordan St. Clair

Who is Jordan St. Clair???

(Pilot)

Jackie Faraday drove along the Los Angeles freeway with her car's top down.

The way God intended convertibles to be driven in L.A.

As she took the exit to the surface street in front of the studio's main entrance, she thought about how she ended up in "show biz".

It started with corporate downsizing in the Commercial Technology Sector. Then another cubicle job courtesy of her Project Management certification. Then more downsizing in the Defense Technology Sector. Finally, on a lark she had applied to ZBS TV/Paradox Motion Pictures Studios.

With her first show business job in the rear view and her second assignment at the studio in front of her, she felt good pulling onto the studio lot, driving among buildings to arrive at building #170; a nondescript structure that looked like a small three bedroom house. With bars on the windows. And a very sturdy front door with a sign that said "PROJECT SUPPORT".

Two out of four assigned parking spaces remained empty in front of the building. In the rightmost parking space was what looked like a new unmarked minivan.

She parked in her assigned slot, grabbed her purse, a pair of sneakers, and walked up to what she assumed was the official entrance to the building. She knew the building's location only because she was shown a studio site map when she interviewed for the job.

As she stepped inside, she saw a large entry room complete with a sofa and a magazine rack full of current magazines. The literature was much better than she had ever seen in any doctor's office.

She walked farther into the building, noting a door on the left marked "SECURITY" as being closed, and an adjacent office's door standing wide open. She peeked into the open office and saw a woman she assumed to be one of her new coworkers clicking away at a computer keyboard.

Jackie turned and walked to an office directly across from the occupied office. The door to this one was marked "MS. FARADAY" with official but not too expensive signage. Opening the door, she noticed her first and last name on a desk sign with an additional line just below that read "Executive Administrator".

She sat down in her desk chair and changed her footwear from business flats to sneakers.

"Business casual meet my new pair of running shoes," she said to herself. The sneakers were one of the perks of the job. Travel, meeting celebrities – finally! – being others.

Jackie walked across to the office opposite hers, noting the Security office door was still shut.

The tall, slender woman sitting behind the standard issue office desk didn't notice Jackie as she entered. She remained fixated on her computer screen.

Jackie tapped on her neighbor's office door. The woman behind the desk turned toward Jackie, smiled and walked eagerly around the desk to shake Jackie's hand.

"Hi! Tonya Manning."

"Hi. Jackie Faraday. Looks like we'll be working together."

"Looks like," Tonya said.

Both women were dressed in the same brand and style of sneakers. They grinned at each other, noting the common footwear.

"So," said Tonya, "pretty sweet ride outside." She wiggled her eyebrows as she spoke. "You saw our minivan, right?"

"Oh, yeah," said Jackie. "Now we just need to have a bunch of kids to fill it up!"

"You have any?" asked Tonya.

"No. You?"

"Nope."

"Do you have the keys to the van?" Jackie asked.

"No."

A nearby door opened.

"Maybe the Security Department has them," said Jackie.

They walked to Tonya's doorway and tilted their heads to peek inside the now open Security office.

They hesitated a moment, looking at each other. Jackie moved first. They smiled at each other as they moved forward in an exaggerated, leisurely fashion.

Standing in the doorway, the women took a moment to check out the contents of the Security office.

Much of the room was occupied by a massive desk. The desk's façade appeared to be a single piece of wood. Two guest chairs sat in front of the desk and another beside a wall across from the desk corner nearest the door. Multiple metal storage containers and filing cabinets stood against the wall on the other side of the room. On the desk was a nameplate that read, "Ms. St. Clair" on the first line and "Security Officer" on the line just below.

Sitting in an expensive winged office chair, was a tiny, dark haired woman in her mid-thirties. Her hair was pulled back and she wore a pair of transition sunglasses through which one could barely make out her eyes.

Her elbows were propped on her desktop, fingers forming a steeple. Her gaze was directed at a corner of the room to her right as Jackie and Tonya quietly entered the room.

Her blouse was a sea blue, her face set like stone, frozen in concentration.

The woman's gaze shifted to the two women who had just entered her office and softened to a smile as she leaned back and her hands went palms down on her desk.

"Hello. Sorry. I was pondering an impending economic apocalypse."

Walking around the desk's side nearest the door, still wearing her glasses, she reached out and shook Jackie and Tonya's hands.

"I'm Jordan St. Clair. I'll be your security detail," Jordan said, smiling and gazing up at both significantly taller women. Jordan looked to be barely five feet tall. With her shoes on. Jackie, though a few inches shorter than Tonya, still felt like a giant.

Both Jackie and Tonya forced a smile to avoid gaping at the petite woman wearing dark pants, black athletic work shoes, and a gun.

Around Jordan's waist, in addition to the gun, were multiple accessory pouches and what looked to be an expandable baton. A large pocket knife was clipped inside one of her pants pockets. Despite her size, her gaze was confident and unflinching.

"Nice to meet you," Jackie and Tonya said almost in unison. They backed out of Jordan's office together. Jordan returned to her chair.

Jackie held her right hand in the air at the height of Jordan's head as she and Tonya returned to Tonya's office.

"I know," mouthed Tonya and she shut her office door after they were both inside.

Jackie sat down in one of Tonya's two guest chairs while Tonya seated herself behind her desk.

"She's so tiny," said Jackie.

"I know," Tonya said, resting her head on her right hand above her desk. "What do we do? She's got a gun but she's just so small."

"Let's call The Boss Man," said Jackie.

"Good idea," Tonya said and she turned to the phone on her desk and started punching buttons. "Let's get some info on this ... strange little person. Was it just me or did her eyebrows seem to kinda move around and change shape while we were talking?"

"You noticed that, too?" Jackie said. "I thought it was the light or I was hallucinating. We need someone bigger. And cuter. And preferably single."

Tonya grinned and nodded as the other phone rang.

The phone was answered by an office administrator and the call transferred to The Manager.

"Hello! How's your first day going, ladies?"

"Great!" said Tonya.

"Really well!" Jackie said.

"Fantastic! I have a special assignment for you three. But you called me. What's up?"

"Weeelll," said Jackie, "we had a question about our security detail."

There was a pause as Jackie waited for The Manager to respond.

"Sure. Is Jordan in her office?" he asked.

"Yeah, she's here," said Jackie. "When we heard we would have security on premises, we expected someone bigger."

"And more than one," Tonya added.

"And more than one," Jackie agreed. "Definitely more than one."

The Manager paused again.

"Look ladies, I know she may not look like much …"

Jackie couldn't stop herself.

"She's barely five feet tall, sir!"

"I know, I know, but trust me, Ms. Faraday.

"Jordan St. Clair is five feet of trouble.

"She comes highly recommended by some very top notch people," The Manager continued. "Give her a try. I'm sure she'll grow on you.

"In the meantime, I need you to run over to Naomi Acosta's house."

"The TV star?" asked Jackie.

"One and the same. She's having some … personal issues that I believe you three can help with. I emailed the details to Jordan," The Manager said. Tonya sat back in her chair and nodded happily.

There was a knock at Tonya's office door and both women jumped.

"Good luck, ladies!" The Manager said, ending the call from his phone.

Jackie opened the door to see Jordan wearing a dark blazer, a security officer hat, and carrying two large, bulging duffle bags suspended from her shoulders, one bag on either side.

Jordan grinned up at Jackie, dangling a key fob in one hand.

"Who wants to be the 'chauffeur'?" Jordan asked.

"Shotgun!" Tonya said.

Jackie turned as Tonya came around the desk and joined Jackie near the doorway.

"Lucky you," said Jordan as she handed the key fob to Jackie and then headed for the building's exit.

"Everybody buckle up!" Jordan said.

Jackie took the driver's seat with Jordan sitting immediately behind her. Tonya got her wish and rode in the minivan's front passenger seat.

"What are we going to do when we get there?" asked Tonya.

"Some basic animal control and errand running," Jordan said.

"Animal control?" said Jackie with concern in her voice.

Jackie thought she might be doing way too much yelling on the first day of her new job. Surely not everyone at ZBS/Paradox had to run the Project Support gauntlet. She had seen normal-looking people on the studio lot. Some even used familiar project management terminology.

"I've got it under control," said Jordan. "I think. I've never really done this specific type of work before. I'm not sure about the right dosage in the darts."

Tonya ignored the last part of Jordan's statement and looked at the van's rear seat.

"Is that why you brought the big dog carrier box?" asked Tonya.

"Yep," Jordan said, rummaging through one of her duffle bags. "And this." Jordan waved a large handgun in the air.

Jackie looked in the rear view mirror. "How many guns do you have?"

"Just the two at the moment. This one is the tranquilizer gun."

"So what are you planning to shoot?" Tonya asked.

"It's a sssecret," Jordan said, snickering.

"I'll let Ms. Acosta tell you. I don't want to ruin the surprise."

Jackie glanced at Tonya and Tonya returned the look and added a shrug.

Naomi Acosta's three bedroom house was … well, it was medium sized. Certainly not too large. But very well organized.

Ms. Acosta wasn't a very large person herself the three women noticed as she rolled two suitcases toward the front door after loudly inviting the three women into her house without answering her front door in person. One of the suitcases flew open, dumping part of the contents on her foyer floor.

Out of the pile of clothing and see-through underwear, rolled a shiny metal object with a round tip.

The three women of Project Support smiled.

"It's so shiny," Tonya said as Jordan moved in for a closer look. Naomi threw everything back into the suitcase, forgetting to close and lock the suitcase. All three women peered into the open piece of luggage.

Realizing what was happening, Naomi turned to face the Project Support Team.

"Hey!" she said.

The Team backed up.

As Naomi zipped the suitcase shut she said, "I'm a good Jewish mother. Who is also dating a musician. He's also experimental.

"Please don't tell my mom."

"We're not judging," said Jackie while Tonya pretended to stare at something elsewhere on the floor. Meanwhile, Jordan was rifling through one of her duffle bags.

"We at Project Support," Jackie continued, "we can keep secrets. Confidentiality is part of our organizational mission statement. We have your back."

Jordan rejoined the three other women.

"And your front," Jordan said, offering the contents of her hands to Ms. Acosta. In one hand, was a tube of personal lubricant and the other hand contained a small box of condoms.

Naomi approached Jordan.

Jordan smiled.

Naomi hesitated, her hand outstretched but not quite making contact with either of Jordan's hands.

Jordan stepped closer.

"Go on. Take the lube."

Jordan put the tube in Naomi's hand and closed Naomi's hand around its contents.

"No judgment," said Jordan, backing away.

"This is a Judgment-Free Zone," said Jackie, as she and Tonya raised their hands in the air.

Naomi looked at all three women as if they were helpful, escaped lunatics.

"Whatever," said Naomi. "Just get the guitar strings and leave them with my agent. You have her contact info.

"Oh, and good luck with the snake. I don't know where it is, but the house isn't that big. Bye!" and Naomi exited the house, pulling the front door shut behind her.

"Snake?!" said Tonya. Jackie smiled, realizing she wasn't the one who lost it this time.

Jackie and Tonya looked at Jordan who was, again, rummaging around in her duffle bags after pitching the box of condoms into the one on the right. Jordan stood up smiling and holding an animal control pole with a hoop of vinyl covered cable on one end.

"Tonya, could you please bring in the box from the van?" Jordan asked.

"Roger that," Tonya said, offering a mock salute before leaving the house to fetch the large plastic box.

"And what do I do?" asked Jackie.

"You get this," Jordan said, handing Jackie the control pole.

Tonya returned, carrying the large crate with both hands. Jackie adjusted the size of the loop a few times until Jordan smiled and said, "That looks about right."

"Now what?" asked Tonya, setting the box on the floor.

"Now you two go that way, toward the bedrooms, and I'll take the den, living room, and dining room side of the house. If you see something, just yell and I'll come running," Jordan said, shaking the tranquilizer gun in the air.

"Is the snake poisonous?" Tonya asked.

Jackie switched her attention from the pole in her hands to Jordan.

"Nah, it's just a big ol' constrictor of some kind. Which reminds me."

Jordan reached into one of the duffle bags and retrieved a large, fixed blade knife. She attached it to her gun belt. "Just in case it grabs hold of anyone or gets hungry," she said.

Jackie and Tonya looked at each other and then headed toward the bedrooms. Jordan, holding the tranquilizer gun in front of her, headed in the opposite direction after taking a look around the foyer.

Tonya and Jackie were cautiously searching the second bedroom and just about to work up the nerve to look under the bed when they heard Jordan yell, "Got it!"

The two women rushed back to the foyer, intending to cross to the other side of the house, but both skidded to a stop when they caught sight of Jordan flying backwards through the air, this scene being framed by the entryway to the other side of the house.

There was a crash and before entering the living room, they heard Jordan say, "Don't got it."

Taking a couple of deep breaths, Jackie and Tonya rushed into the room adjacent to the foyer. Jackie held the control stick like a spear and Tonya raised the dog carrier above her head like a colossus holding a boulder.

As the three women leaned back on the sofa, they were relieved to hear Naomi Acosta tell Jackie some good news.

"I hated that snake," said Naomi. "It gave me the creeps the first time it slithered across my legs. He can get another one. Thanks for trying though. Just clean up the mess and all is well. And forgotten.

"Oh, but don't forget the guitar strings."

"You got it!" Jackie said into her cell phone. "Nice talking to you, Ms. Acosta."

All three women sighed at the same time.

Tonya snickered and the other two women looked at her.

"How about new belts for all of us? Anyone know a good butcher?" asked Tonya.

The others snickered.

Jordan eased herself off the couch with the tranquilizer gun in hand and fired the gun.

"You can never be too careful," Jordan said.

"Amen to that, sister," said Jackie. Tonya giggled.

"All yours, ladies," Jordan said.

After loading the pet carrier into the van, the three women resumed their previous seating arrangement. The next stop was Animal Control followed by a music store as yet to be determined by Tonya and the minivan's onboard navigational system.

"The guitar strings are over there," said Tonya, pointing while making full use of her height.

As they walked to the opposite side of the store, Jordan quietly broke off in another direction, stopping to peer through a rehearsal room window at a head bobbing, hair throwing band in the throes of metal ecstasy.

"I think there are different kinds of strings for the different kinds of guitars," Tonya said.

"You know, some need to be plugged in, some don't," she said, looking at a wall full of guitar strings.

"Judging by that snake, I'm guessing his owner is not into folk music. My vote is for 'electric guitar'," Jackie said.

They waved down a store employee and after a few minutes of instruction and head scratching, the two women purchased several of what were supposed to be the best strings available. Courtesy of their ZBS company credit card of course.

As Tonya grabbed the bag of guitar strings, she asked, "Where's Jordan?"

Starting in the areas nearest the front door, Tonya and Jackie made their way toward the instruction and rehearsal rooms. They had checked the women's restroom and agreed they didn't know anything about their coworker (yet) that would cause them to search the men's room as well. They stopped at the rehearsal room where the metal band was playing.

They saw Jordan, harmonica in hand, bobbing her head not quite enough to dislodge her security officer's hat, but still matching the timing of the other musicians.

Jordan looked up and noticed Jackie and Tonya staring through the rehearsal room window. Their faces almost touched the glass and their mouths were open.

Jordan jerked her head in their direction and waved at the band as she moved to leave the room.

She closed the door behind her as a wall of sonic metal mayhem flew out the room. She tapped the harmonica against her thigh and placed it in one of the pouches on her gun belt.

Jackie and Tonya stared at Jordan, Jackie with her arms crossed and Tonya holding the bag of guitar strings.

Jordan looked up at them, noting their curious stares.

"What? They're my regular Saturday night band. It doesn't pay that much, but I need the exposure."

Jackie and Tonya looked at each other as they followed the shortest member of their team out of the store.

Jackie smiled as the three women rode back to work.

In her mind, as first days go on a new job, things had gone pretty well.

"I had some excitement," she thought to herself, "and I went shopping and spent someone else's money. Not bad at …"

"STOP THE VAN!" Jordan shouted.

Jackie pulled the minivan over. Tonya and Jackie stared – yet again – as Jordan swiftly exited the van and ran across the street to join a mime flash mob that was already in progress. The mob was led by a man whose face was painted white, his eyebrows and mouth highlighted with black lines. He and all the participants wore pink shirts. The whole performance played out in a plaza created by a vacant space between buildings on the other side of the six lane street.

"Cool," said Tonya. "Cancer awareness."

Jackie nodded. "Wanna join in?"

Tonya smiled and nodded. She and Jackie left the minivan and crossed the street.

"I didn't think they still did these," said Tonya.

"It's a 'retro' mime flash mob," Jackie said with a deadpan look that morphed into a big smile.

"A 'retro' flash mob," said Tonya.

"For cancer," Jackie said.

Jackie and Tonya joined the crowd and mimicked Jordan as Jordan copied the leader's movements.

"She's so good," whispered Tonya.

"I know," Jackie whispered back.

As Jordan, Jackie, and Tonya pretended to be thrown backwards by an invisible wind, Jordan turned and lassoed the other two women with invisible ropes. Jordan turned, bowed herself and walked into the imaginary gale "dragging" the other two women with her as the three of them crossed the street toward the minivan. The three women broke character as they were midway across the street. They all laughed as they drove away in the minivan, but Jackie wondered to herself:

"Who is Jordan St. Clair?"

4

Jackie slipped into a guest chair in front of Jordan's desk as the Project Support Team awaited a call from The Manager. Tonya positioned herself atop Jordan's desk at the corner nearest the door.

Even with Jordan's slightly darkened eyeglasses obstructing a clear view of Jordan's eyes, Jackie could tell Jordan was not happy with Tonya's choice of perches.

The first few weeks had been pretty mundane since the whole snake thing. The three women had gone to lunch together occasionally, though it was usually just Jackie and Tonya during these events.

"What do you suppose she does in there?" Tonya asked during one of the luncheons sans Jordan.

"Oils her guns, counts her bullets, sharpens her knives ... you know, girly stuff," Jackie said. "She's got little muscles, but I bet they're all hard as a rock."

For the past few weeks they had carried paperwork around the studio lot and the city; important paperwork, but just paperwork. They would ask Jordan through her closed office door if she wanted to join them.

"More paperwork?" Jordan would ask through the door.

Jackie and Tonya would answer in the affirmative.

Jordan would remain behind.

Now, Tonya sat on the edge of Jordan's desk, looking at her nails, idly moving one of her legs back and forth.

Jackie tried to make eye contact with Tonya, but Tonya had switched her focus to the floor.

"Your ass is on my desk," said Jordan.

Tonya looked at Jackie. Jackie smiled slightly and shrugged just a little as she looked at the floor and leaned her head on one of her hands.

Tonya stood up, turned to face the spot she had occupied on Jordan's desk and wiped the surface with her hand.

"Now you're wiping your ass all over my desk," said Jordan.

Jackie prevented herself from laughing out loud, but couldn't help shaking during the effort.

"I give up," said Tonya and she sat down in a guest chair near the office wall located on Jordan's left.

Jackie breathed deeply, wiped away a tear and sent a sympathetic look Tonya's way.

"St. Clair," said Jackie. Jordan looked at Jackie.

Was that a playful smile on Jordan's face?

"That's a pretty name," Jackie said. Tonya nodded.

"What's your middle name?" asked Jackie.

Jordan held up her right hand's middle finger.

"It's French," she said.

Tonya's mouth fell open. The rest of her face was devoted to puzzlement. A similar look was on Jackie's face, but Jackie's mouth remained shut. Jackie told herself she had tried and to just let it go, as did Tonya a few moments later.

The phone on Jordan's desk rang.

Jordan tapped a button on her phone.

"Hello?" The Manager called out from his end.

"Hi! We're all here!" Jackie said.

"Good! So I'm going to get right to it. There are a couple of special tasks I have for you three."

"Yes?" asked Jordan, leaning toward the phone.

"There's been a small accident on the lot. No one was hurt. But Jimmy Galewski and his three buddies need a ride," said The Manager.

"Jimmy Galewski from that show about the science geeks?" asked Tonya of Jordan's phone.

"One and the same. And the three other passengers are also stars on the show," The Manager replied.

"Don't any of them have their own car? Can't they just call a cab?" Jackie asked.

"They all have cars. They just happened to ride to the studio today with Jimmy. The studio would like you three to give them a ride to Jake Paddock's house. As a goodwill gesture," said The Manager.

Jackie looked at Tonya and Jordan. Jackie said, "Why? They're already paying them truckloads of money. Isn't that enough goodwill?"

The three women heard The Manager sigh.

"The studio feels bad because the studio accidentally blew up Galewski's car," The Manager said. "That was the 'accident' part.

"They feel like they owe him a ride to his buddy's house. And more."

"How did he get his car blown up?" Tonya asked.

"It was parked in the wrong spot. The Special Effects department towed it because they were expecting the car parked in that exact spot to be used for a movie scene where a car gets blown up.

"Galewski maintains he parked his car in his normal VIP parking space."

"Can't they just look at security videos to see what happened?" asked Jackie.

"They could," said The Manager, "but they don't want to ruffle any feathers. Plus at this point, what does it matter? His car's in pieces, he gets a new one on Monday plus some TLC from the Project Support Department."

"We're glad to do it," Jackie said and the other women nodded in agreement.

"It'll be our pleasure," Tonya said.

"I'll email Jordan the details and I'm writing up a full description of your afternoon task. They'll both get you out of the office. Should be fun! Good bye," said The Manager and he hung up.

"So where are we going to, Jordan?" asked Jackie.

Jordan looked at her computer monitor situated on a small table in a space between two large bookshelves behind her desk.

"Nowhere near that movie set, hopefully," Jordan muttered while staring at the monitor.

"Yeah, okay," she said, turning around, "we're going on a short ride to Jimmy's VIP parking spot to pick him and the boys up, and then we get to see how the rich and famous live. Again. After that, we'll come back here, take a lunch break and then be tied up for most of the afternoon."

"No snakes expected at Jake's house?" Tonya said, smiling.

Jordan and Jackie both smiled as well.

"Not at this point," said Jordan.

Jimmy Galewski, Jake Paddock, Seth Hurvitz, and Kabal Narong stood in Jimmy's assigned parking space, texting like crazy as the Project Support minivan pulled up perpendicular to the parking space's entry point.

A passenger side sliding door opened and the four men entered the van.

Jimmy took the bucket seat separated from Jordan's by a small armrest/storage bin. Tonya noted he was several inches taller than Jordan, but not as tall as herself. He and Jackie were about tied height-wise.

Making themselves comfortable, Seth, Jake (his long legs resting in the space between Jordan and Jimmy) and Kabal buckled themselves in from port to starboard, respectively, in the rear seat.

As they drove through the parking lot, Jordan said, "Sorry we couldn't provide a ride in something nicer. My car is too small."

Jimmy looked up from his phone. "What do you drive?"

As they neared the studio lot's exit, Jordan pointed to a red Porsche.

"How'd you afford that?" asked Jimmy.

Jordan turned to him. Jimmy felt uncomfortable receiving her full attention.

"A congressman gave it to me," said Jordan.

Jimmy's eyebrows rose.

Jackie turned the van into traffic trying not to jostle her celebrity passengers but also listened to the story being told behind her.

"I got him a hooker," she said.

"Then he married the hooker."

The conversation over, she returned to looking out the window on her side of the van.

The remaining celebrity occupants of the van remained quietly stunned.

"Ain't love grand," said Jimmy.

Tonya couldn't resist looking his way. She said, "Do you need a hooker?"

"No, I'm good," Jimmy said. Tonya shifted her gaze to the minivan's back seat.

"I'm gay," Jake Paddock said.

From the driver's seat, Jackie said, "This is L.A. You know that's not a problem, right?"

Realizing he didn't actually know these women, Jake responded, "No, I'm good. Really."

Jake grinned at his co-stars sitting on either side, wiggling his eyebrows.

"We're married!" they said in unison.

"This is L.A. You know that's not a problem, right?" Jake said to his co-stars.

"We're good, too!" Kabal said and Seth quickly nodded in agreement as he turned his attention back to his phone.

"Really. We're good. We're all good," said Seth.

As the minivan traveled up the nearest freeway's on ramp, Jordan looked at Jimmy and asked, "So what's Chuck Lorre really like?"

Jimmy looked up from his phone.

"You don't want to know."

The rest of the trip was uneventful.

The yellow Hummer rolled to a stop about 200 yards from the block wall marking a remote edge of the studio's property line.

"None too soon," Jackie thought, concluding any further travel over mounds of dirt and grass would have rattled her insides loose. Tonya had been concerned as well, tightly gripping whatever part of the interior seemed most likely to prevent unexpected bodily harm.

But not Jordan.

"Turn the car so it's parallel to the wall," said Jordan.

"So we can take cover?" asked Tonya.

"No, so you can pee without being seen."

Jordan dug inside one of the duffle bags in the seat next to her and pulled out two orange trowels. Holding them handle-up, a roll of toilet paper adorned each handle.

"Your own DIY restrooms, ladies," said Jordan, smiling.

"Where's yours?" asked Tonya as she and Jackie reached for the trowels.

Jordan tipped her head to the right. A bright orange bucket sat behind Tonya's seat.

"I get a bucket. With a lid. I'm special," said Jordan.

"Whatever," said Jackie.

"A vehicle to hide behind is one of the benefits of borrowing a Security big rig," Jordan said. "Plus it has an intimidating presence."

"But nobody's going to see us doing our business behind the car, right?" said Tonya.

"Right," said Jordan. "We're to observe this part of the property line for the next 3 hours because it's one of the sections without cameras.

"If anyone from the studio comes our way, I'll hear about it on the walkie.

"We need to move the rest of our stuff closer to the wall though."

Over the course of the next half hour the three women dragged rolling crates, lawn chairs, assorted boxes, and a case of bottled water to a location closer to the wall.

Jackie and Tonya lowered themselves into lawn chairs situated under umbrellas.

"That was a chore. Now what do we do? Just keep an eye out for crazed nerds and yell at them?" asked Jackie.

"A little more than just that," Jordan replied. "During the next three hours, there will be lots of interviews and photos taken of major film stars working in the latest superhero movie produced by Paradox.

"Every nerd in this city ... every crazy nerd in this city ... will want to grab a picture or autograph."

Jordan began opening plastic crates and cardboard boxes. Her coworkers continued reclining as Jordan pulled objects from different containers and appeared to be assembling something as Jackie and Tonya watched.

"Do you need any help?" asked Tonya.

"No, I've got it," Jordan replied. She walked over to Tonya, bypassing Jackie, and handed Tonya a paintball rifle.

"This," Jordan said, "is your 'nerd dispersal weapon'. It has 200 paintballs loaded, and a CO_2 bottle that will last you quite a while.

"I'll bring over more paintballs, but the idea is that we discourage any incursions today and send a message. Especially if they start to swarm."

Jackie raised her hand.

"Are we trying to kill them?" she asked.

"No," said Jordan. "Your weapons' pressure settings are set to just sting. They'll get a light bruise at most."

"However," she continued, "after I shoot them, some of the 'boy' nerds may be leaving as 'girl' nerds."

Jackie and Tonya exchanged looks.

"Maybe just Tonya and I should do the shooting," Jackie said as she took her rifle from Jordan.

Jordan look at Jackie and Tonya.

"Suit yourself. You might want to practice a little though," said Jordan.

Jordan sat down in her own lawn chair and opened a word-jumble puzzle book and began circling words, apparently no longer interested in the task at hand. Jackie and Tonya practiced, doing their best to make the block wall more colorful than when they had arrived.

Half an hour later, Jackie and Tonya had grown proficient with their weapons and were in the process of reloading when Jordan, without looking up from her book, commented, "You're getting better. I'm impressed."

"So when's the action really start?" asked Tonya.

Jordan and Jackie looked at Tonya. Tonya sounded very eager to do some damage.

"Soon," said Jordan. "First, they'll see us here and … oops. There's your first customers. Look alive snipers."

Three people peered over the wall, only their heads and hands showing. Jackie and Tonya fired off multiple rounds in rapid succession. The trio of trespassers ducked down, their faces splattered with paint.

"I like shooting at nerds," Tonya said, grinning.

Jackie and Jordan laughed.

"You're a maniac. You have a new calling," said Jordan as she searched for the next word in her book.

Ten minutes went by and the three women could make out a large number of voices on the other side of the wall.

"They're going to swarm soon," Jordan said.

"Then what do we do?" asked Jackie.

"We send a message. Excuse me. I need to use my bucket. Keep an eye out."

A few more minutes passed and then what looked like at least thirty people began climbing over the wall simultaneously. Jackie and Tonya starting firing but their targets ignored any physical or psychological discomfort.

As the first trespasser touched down on studio property, Jordan whipped out a tranquilizer rifle from a nearby duffle bag, knelt down on one knee while taking aim, and shot a brightly colored dart into the trespasser's hip. The male nerd hit the ground and went to sleep.

Jackie turned to Jordan and asked, "Are you sure that was safe?"

"Note the crowd reaction," Jordan said, putting another dart in the rifle and walking toward the wall.

The remainder of the trespassers were retreating over the wall. Jordan waved her rifle in the air. Only the snoring nerd was left on studio property. She walked back to Tonya and Jackie, returning her rifle to the duffle bag and sat down in her lawn chair.

"I'm better with people than snakes," said Jordan.

"Lots of training?" asked Tonya.

"Lots of practice," said Jordan.

About an hour later, the nerd on the ground began to stir. Jordan noticed the movement and smiled. Jackie and Tonya wanted to ask if they should help, but they sensed Jordan had a plan.

As the slightly overweight young man gathered the strength to sit up and lean back against the wall, Jordan fetched her orange bucket and carried it toward the groggy trespasser.

Jackie and Tonya watched as she approached the bleary-eyed young man, shaking their heads back and forth.

Jordan removed the bucket's lid and poured its contents on the young man's head. He screamed and stumbled toward the wall.

"Let me give you a boost," said Jordan said as she helped the young man begin his ascent, carefully avoiding any of her homemade weapon dripping from him.

Satisfied the former trespasser had made it over the wall, Jordan put the lid back on the bucket and walked to where Jackie and Tonya sat laughing.

"Any more trouble and there's more where that came from," Jordan said and then walked past her coworkers to the opposite side of the SUV.

"This is the most fun I have ever had at work," said Tonya. Her eyes glittered and a big smile spread across her face. Jackie nodded and they made a toast with their water bottles.

Jordan returned to her lawn chair and her book. No more trespassers made an appearance within their visual range the remainder of the afternoon.

5

"Did you do that?" Jackie asked.

"Do I look like an elephant?" said Jordan.

Jackie, Tonya, and Jordan stared at the expensive foreign car covered hood to bumper with large balls of feces. The car was owned by comedic television actor Brian Cramer.

"Why do you think it's from an elephant?" asked Tonya, tugging at the sleeves of her white coveralls with her gloved hands. Jackie was making similar adjustments to her identical attire. They each held large plastic shovels in one of their hands.

"And also, why don't you have to do this?" Jackie asked through her face mask, a fashion accessory also worn by Tonya.

"First," said Jordan, "I've been around elephants before ..."

"Like at the zoo?" asked Tonya.

"No," Jordan said, "and second, I am 'Security'. I am here to make sure you clean the car safely without injuring yourselves, the car, or the studio's integrity.

"You two are in charge of the ... high brown, intellectual stuff," Jordan said, smiling and emphasizing the word "stuff".

Jordan sat down in a lawn chair and watched from a respectable distance while Jackie and Tonya filled plastic bags with excrement and hauled them to a nearby dumpster. Jackie and Tonya felt grateful washing the car by hand was not on their "to do" list. That fun was reserved for the folks at a nearby car wash.

They were working on the roof, trying not to scratch it, when Brian Cramer arrived via a studio VIP golf cart. Brian stepped out of the cart and the golf cart's driver drove away as soon as his passenger exited the vehicle.

Jordan sipped on a blue slushie as Cramer slowly approached his dung-covered vehicle.

He flung his hands up in the air and let them settle on his hips while he shook his head. His movements seemed to mimic his on-air neurotic persona.

"This is great!" Brian shouted. "They told me not to come see it, but I had to. I don't believe it!"

He turned to Jordan. She put her cup on the armrest of her chair, pulling the straw from her mouth and gave him a sympathetic blue smile.

"Who would do something like this?" he said and shook his head again.

Tonya and Jackie took the opportunity to pause from shoveling poop and walked around to a position near the hood of the car. Cramer backed away, thinking they might be fans of some kind who happened to be wearing poop-smeared coveralls. The two women, seeing his discomfort, stopped.

"We think it was the same person or persons who moved Jimmy Galewski's car so his car would be blown up," said Jordan.

"You're joking," Tonya said through her mask.

"Nope. The folks in Main Security are calling him 'The Phantom'," said Jordan.

"Well, you two are doing a great job cleaning this up," Brian said, smiling and feeling relieved Jackie and Tonya had ceased their approach.

"We have an extra set of coveralls if you'd like to help," said Jackie with a slightly wicked smile that leaked out around the edges of her mask.

"And we also have matching booties!" Tonya said, raising one of her feet in the air for a moment to show off her foot apparel which were no longer completely white for more than one reason.

Jackie smiled at Cramer and nodded.

"Oh no. That's okay. I'm a TV star," he said, backing away, just realizing the golf cart driver had abandoned him.

A shiny luxury car pulled up and parked nearby. The front passenger-side door opened. The driver was one of Cramer's female co-stars on his current television show. Her name was Donna Morgan and, though in her late sixties, was still quite striking and apparently sexually active from the look she gave Brian Cramer.

"So, Brian," Donna said. "Would you like a lift?"

Tonya looked at Jackie.

"Doesn't she play his mom?" asked Tonya.

"Yep. This is about to get kinda twisted."

She and Tonya backed away to the side of the vehicle farthest from Cramer.

"Play your cards right and Momma will be extra nice to you," said Donna.

Brian stared at the open car door and considered the invitation for a ride and a whole lot more.

Behind him there was a slurping sound.

Cramer's head turned toward the sound.

Jordan held up an empty cup.

"Out of slushie," she said.

Tonya and Jackie's eyebrows went up. Donna Morgan was still leaning over when Jordan pulled out an unopened bottle of water from a cooler sitting next to her and proceeded to open the bottle. She also pulled an extra set of coveralls and booties from a bag near her feet and laid them on the armrest of her lawn chair.

"You know," Brian said, "it looks like these two ladies could sure use an extra hand. I think I'll just let them drive me home. After we clean up the mess of course."

"Suit yourself," Ms. Morgan called out. The passenger door shut and the car pulled away. Brian Cramer sighed.

"I owe you all slushies," he said.

"You want a shovel or do you just want to hold the bag?" asked Jackie.

"Which job has less splatter?"

"We'll fling gently," Jackie said as she came around the car and handed him an empty bag.

6

"Hit me, barkeep," said Jordan.

Jackie repositioned her night vision goggles and reached behind herself for a bottle of wine. She filled Jordan's wine glass about a third full.

"Thanks."

"Don't mention it," said Jackie.

The three of them sat in the dark atop the roof belonging to the tallest building on the lot. Their surveillance/Phantom Search had started after dinner and sunset.

Tonya rubbed her face.

"Does anyone else's face itch from the camo paint?" Tonya asked.

"Yeah. But it goes so well with the ninja clothes," Jackie said.

"Don't forget the hats," said Jordan. "It's actually just basic tactical clothing. No ninja pajamas."

"I love all the pockets," Tonya said, looking down at her pants.

"These night vision goggles are so cool!" said Jackie. "You can zoom in and out ... and in and out."

"I know!" said Tonya.

Jordan shook her head and peered out across the studio property and adjacent sections of L.A.

"I can see all over L.A.," Tonya said. "I can see Chuck Lorre sitting on the toilet!"

Jackie looked where Tonya was pointing and fiddled with the magnification level of her goggles.

"I can see him, too!" said Jackie.

"I think he lives in Malibu," Jordan said.

"Oh. Well he could be sitting on someone else's toilet," said Tonya.

"Wait. I think it's that one female comedian," said Jackie.

"You're right," Tonya said. "And she's shaving. On the toilet."

"What's she shaving?" asked Jordan.

"Her face, you pervert," Tonya said. "Hairy old ladies. You gotta love 'em."

"No, no actually you don't," said Jackie.

Jordan shook her head again, swirled her glass gently, and sipped.

Another hour and they went home without any evildoers observed. The Phantom, if such a person existed, went undetected that night by the three women.

7

"Sooo, exactly when did you first learn your son wanted to be a …" started Jackie as she watched Ellen Franklin's eyes begin to water.

"A mime," finished Jordan.

She took a seat next to Ellen on the couch. Ellen held a tissue in one hand and hugged a small, but expensive looking pillow to her chest with the other. Jordan gave Ellen a reassuring touch on the shoulder.

"It's okay. Go ahead," Jordan said.

Tonya leaned forward slightly in her chair. She sat in a comfortable chair in the Franklin's mansion which was full of nice things and comfortable seating. Jackie tried to smile sympathetically. It was hard after all the layoffs she had been through to feel sorry for someone who lived so well. But she didn't enjoy seeing Ellen's pain either.

"It started with books and DVD's. My husband, Lawrence, wanted David to become a producer like Larry.

"Or maybe a lawyer. Something, anything, on the business side of show business," Ellen said.

"But David wanted something else," said Jordan.

Ellen wiped the corners of her eyes.

"Exactly. He's 18. He has a right to make his own decisions. It's just that we haven't heard from him.

"We know he's alive. His credit card is being used. His cell phone is in use. We just want him back home."

"And we want this handled discreetly," said Ellen looking at Jackie and Tonya. Ellen noticed Jordan's gun for the first time. Jordan took note of Ellen's gaze.

"I'm just here for added protection. These two handle all the diplomacy issues. Everything will be handled discreetly. We're professionals," Jordan said.

"We'll be very discreet," said Jackie.

"Unless your son turns out to be a snake," thought Tonya.

Jordan gently rubbed Ellen's shoulder.

"We'll let ourselves out. You be well," said Jordan. "We'll give you a call when we find him."

"And we'll alert the security firm you've contracted with to bring him home."

"I don't want him hurt," Ellen said.

"We wouldn't dream of it," said Jordan.

Tonya and Jackie's shoes clicked against the expensive floors as they left the mansion. As usual, Jordan kept pace with the taller women with seemingly little effort and without making a sound.

"She glides," thought Tonya.

As they walked to the van, Tonya glanced back at the house and said, "The Rich are so different."

"Yep," said Jackie as she opened the driver's door of the van. "The major difference is that you could park my apartment in their garage."

The three women buckled into their seats and Jordan spoke.

"Losing your son, your plans for what he would have become, is a kind of death. It's the death of a dream. It's seeing your son as he is rather than who you thought he was, who he was supposed to be. Her husband told her it was her fault her son wanted to become a mime, that Ellen was too quiet."

"You seem to be taking this personally," said Tonya.

"I just hate to see good people hurt. When we get to the mime school, I'm going to kick some silent ass."

"Greater L.A. Mime Academy here we come," Jackie said.

Pulling into the parking lot of G.L.A.M.A., Tonya remarked the building was bigger than she expected.

"Mime is a basic skill for a lot of comedians and actors. The school doesn't have any trouble finding new students," Jordan said. "Their academic credits transfer to most major universities."

Entering through the front glass doors, the three women saw that the Public wasn't allowed to see much from the foyer. The sign-in sheet on the counter and posters on the walls made it look like an ordinary business office.

"We're looking for David Franklin," Jackie said as the three of them stood at the reception counter. "We need to give him a message."

The man sitting behind the counter in mime makeup and a turtleneck gestured toward a sign on the counter.

"'Try to express yourself using gestures and body movement before speaking'," Tonya read aloud. The mime behind the desk smiled and clapped his gloved hands together in muffled applause. He indicated via hand movements they should continue their end of the conversation.

Jackie gestured toward her coworkers and herself and using two fingers indicated they would like to look around and walk through two swinging doors several feet behind the reception desk. A sign on either door read, "Classes in session. Please be respectful."

The mime smiled again and pointed to the sign-in sheet. Tonya reached for a pen chained to the counter.

"We don't have time for this," said Jordan. "Have a seat, ladies. This won't take long."

Jackie and Tonya backed toward two nearby chairs as Jordan walk around the desk and stared at the startled man for a moment before lunging at him.

The man stood up and attempted to back away, but then Jordan disappeared from view and he appeared to lose his footing.

Tonya started to rise from her chair. Jackie touched her on the arm and looked her in the eye. Tonya sat back down.

Whispers could be heard from the other side of the reception counter. Jackie and Tonya couldn't quite make out the words except when the mime said, "Please."

There was a sound like someone getting spanked and Jordan's head reappeared behind the counter.

"That wasn't so hard. Thank you for your help," said Jordan as she walked around the counter toward Jackie and Tonya. The two women stood up and joined their coworker as Jordan turned to exit the building.

"He switched from 'mime' to 'clown'," Jordan said as they walked to the minivan.

"Why would he do that?" asked Jackie.

"It's the quiet. Some people can't take it," said Jordan. "It's so damn quiet.

"Plus the turtlenecks itch."

Jackie and Tonya looked at each other, unsure how to react.

"How did he switch from mime school to clown college without anyone knowing?" asked Tonya.

"Musta used cash," Jordan said as Jackie started the minivan. "Typical clown college tactic."

"Where to now?" asked Tonya.

"We head over to Floppy Feet, Inc." Jordan said. "I'll give you the directions."

"Floppy Feet, Inc." repeated Jackie.

"It's a private clown college," Jordan said. "Very elitist."

Jackie, Tonya, and Jordan walked into the main rehearsal/performance arena together through a gap in the stands. On either side of the ringed area, there were bleachers. Combined, the seating areas could hold about 150 people.

There were a dozen student clowns standing around on the other side of the circus ring. Most were chatting with each other. A half dozen jugglers practiced a safe distance from the clowns and a lone fire breather practiced several feet from the Project Support Team.

The fire breather spewed flame toward the yellow star marking the circus ring's center. Seeing the three women, the fire breather turned toward them and prepared to demonstrate his talent in their direction.

Before he could eject a stream of fire, Jordan opened her jacket just enough to reveal her gun. The performer redirected his demonstration toward the center of the ring.

Jordan smiled.

On Jackie's left, a portable electric megaphone sat unattended on a barrel. She picked it up and said, "Testing … testing 1-2-3!"

Satisfied with the volume, she continued.

"Attention everyone! Please. Could I have your attention! We're looking for David Franklin. David. Franklin. He's a student here."

Tonya held out her hand. Jackie gave her the megaphone.

"David," said Tonya, "If you're here, we need to talk to you.

"Your mom sent us."

As the last of Tonya's words echoed and faded, two clowns put their heads together on the other side of the ring. The rest of the performers just stared at the three women.

Jackie and Tonya looked at each other and shrugged. Jordan watched the two clowns conversing.

The two clowns stopped talking, took three steps toward the center of the ring and then bolted toward a two person clown car parked just outside the circus ring.

Their oversized shoes squeaked as they ran. They flung open the doors on either side of the vehicle and hopped into the tiny car. A small gasoline-powered engine came to life and its sputter was heard as the car rolled toward curtains on one side of the performance area.

The three women gave chase and made it through the curtains only to see the car and its passengers disappear through a large sunlit opening in the side of the building. A large door rolled down and closed the rectangular entrance just after the car exited the building. The Project Support Team ran through a normal-sized door near the larger exit and found themselves staring at the parking lot. They ran toward their minivan.

"Can they drive that thing on regular streets?" Tonya asked as they entered their vehicle.

"It's L.A." said Jackie.

"Oh, yeah," said Tonya.

"I'm sure it's practically encouraged," Jackie said as they pulled into the street several car lengths behind the much smaller car.

People honked and waved as they passed the two fugitive clowns. The clowns did not respond to the attention and focused on the street ahead.

"Pull up alongside it!" Jordan said.

The minivan's starboard sliding door opened as the clown car swerved toward the larger Project Support vehicle.

"Really?" yelled Jackie.

Tonya rolled down her window so the clowns could actually hear any further shouting from Jackie. The clown car lacked windows on its car doors. A large hole dominated its roof, making it less than ideal to drive if it had been raining. It was clearly an indoor clown car.

"Definitely not meant for the street," Tonya said, looking down at the two clowns through the hole in the roof.

"Hey! Clowns aren't supposed to do that with their middle fingers! At least not while you're in makeup!" Jackie said.

"Right?" asked Jackie of Tonya.

"You tell 'em!" said Tonya.

Jordan leaped from the minivan to the roof of the clown car.

The smaller vehicle's costumed driver turned the steering wheel right and left in an attempt to dislodge Jordan from the roof. The clown car swayed.

Barely.

Jordan reached through the hole in the roof, groping for the steering wheel while keeping her eyes on the road and holding on to the roof with her other hand. She stopped her search and pulled her hand back after it came in contact with something squishy.

She looked at the rubber nose in her hand for a moment before she squeezed it twice. The nose squeaked both times.

Jordan smiled.

She threw the nose away as the clown car rolled through an intersection whose light was yellow. She put both hands on the either side of the roof's opening and, while supporting herself with both arms, dropped the lower part of her body into the car and kicked both men in the head and neck repeatedly until she was sure they were unconscious.

Jordan lowered herself into the vehicle just enough to steer the car to the nearest curb and switched the vehicle's engine off while the unconscious clowns slept.

As the limo with David Franklin and his mother drove away, Jackie, Tonya, and Jordan watched a tow truck driver try to figure out how to attach the clown car to the back of his truck. Clown cars, lacking the right to drive on surface roads in normal traffic, were not towed often. The executive security personnel had called the tow truck to avoid any police involvement.

"Not even in L.A." said Tonya.

"Nope, you can't drive a clown car in regular traffic. Even in L.A." said Jackie. She turned to look at Jordan. "You were amazing!"

"You were!" said Tonya. "That was incredible!"

"Thank you," said Jordan, her arms crossed, watching the tow truck driver scratch his posterior as he further assessed the situation.

"It wasn't my first clown car car chase. And it won't be my last," Jordan said.

Jordan spit in the street, uncrossed her arms, turned, and walked toward the Project Support minivan parked nearby.

Jackie and Tonya followed a few feet behind their one-woman security detail, smiling and shaking their heads.

8

"I guess we can't drink while we're on duty," Jackie said.

"Probably not," said Tonya. "It's nice in here though." She rubbed nearby sections of the limo's interior.

"It is," said Jackie, taking in her surroundings minus the touching. She had heard stories about what people did in these things. It was probably worse than a hotel room.

"No big deal for you, Jord-O?" asked Jackie.

Jordan stared back at her. Jackie decided it was too early in their working relationship for spontaneous nicknames.

"It's not my first time in one," said Jordan. "This one's okay. It's very nice. I've been in better though." She sighed and then continued.

"My phone says we're supposed to deliver a couple of gift baskets after we take Ms. Smith shopping."

"I guess the minivan wasn't good enough for a big TV star," Jackie said.

"Some sort of contractual thing," said Jordan.

"Where are we taking the gift baskets?" asked Tonya.

"To the set of a detective show. The one where the British guy and the actress from that one female samurai movie are the stars."

"A movie star? That's cool," said Tonya.

"Yep. Real groovy," said Jackie. "Here she comes!"

Carrie Smith wore loose clothing, a broad brimmed hat, and sunglasses as she exited the canopied soundstage door.

"At least she opens her own doors," said Jackie to Tonya right before the limo driver materialized and opened the car door for the celebrity.

"Thank you!" said Carrie Smith. Looking at her fellow passengers, she said, "Ready to go shopping with a real live TV star, bitches?"

The Project Support Team smiled and laughed only after Carrie smiled and winked.

Jordan "took point" and walked in front of Carrie Smith's Whole Foods shopping cart as Jackie pushed. Tonya pulled items off the shelf as Carrie pointed to them.

"Oh," said Carrie. "We have to get tampons for Linda."

"Linda Raymond your co-star?" asked Jackie.

"Yep! This way, ladies! Oh, and we have to get 'extra-large'. She's had a couple of kids you know."

Carrie held out her hands in front of her as if holding an inflated balloon.

"Actually," said Jordan, "I heard she had some work down there," and Jordan held her hands out as though holding a deflating balloon and added a whistling sound.

"Huh," said Carrie. "She never told me. Oh and don't let me forget; I have an autographed picture to give you three to hang up in your office."

"Thanks," Jackie said, looking over her shoulder at Tonya as Carrie Smith looked elsewhere.

Jackie and Jordan walked onto the TV show set where the male lead, Jerry Martin, seemed to be having a very earnest conversation with Tonya. Lisa Wong, his co-star stood in the living room section of the set talking to a man with headphones around his neck. Jackie and Jordan each carried a large gift basket.

Jackie looked at Jordan.

"Sound guy?" Jackie asked.

"Or the show's director."

They watched Tonya and Jerry for a moment and then split up. Jackie took her basket to Jerry.

"I just want to make this clear," said Jerry, "I'm not a real detective. It's just a television character. Just like this den we're standing in. It's just another part of a set to make you think we're in a house."

"I know," Tonya said. "I just wanted to know if you had a system for finding your socks. My boyfriends tend to have issues in that area."

Jerry's facial expression switched from confused to happy when he noticed Jackie holding his gift basket.

"For me?"

Jackie held out the basket.

"This is wonderful!" he said.

He turned to Tonya.

"I'm sure you'll find the perfect system. Or a better boyfriend. Any man would be lucky to have you."

He carried his gift basket into the set's kitchen area.

Lisa Wong, who played his associate, gushed over her basket. She and Jordan were about the same height.

Jordan smiled as Jackie and Tonya joined the two of them.

"I'm glad you like it. It's the Studio's way of saying thank you for six great seasons," said Jackie.

"Your show is the best detective show on TV," said Tonya.

"Definitely the best," Jackie said.

"You're so kind!" said Lisa.

"Attention everyone!" said Jackie. "In honor of your sixth successful season, the entire cast and crew will be treated to a catered luncheon at Sophia's Italian Kitchen!"

Everyone within earshot applauded. Ms. Wong handed off her gift basket to a young woman.

While everyone else was talking about lunch, Jordan prowled the living room area. The set was dressed in precise detail, including bookshelves filled with real books and a samurai sword leaning against a wall next to a well-used comfy living room chair.

Jordan pulled the sword from its sheath, exposing the blade just enough to tell if it was real or not.

Jerry Martin came up behind her and leaned against a wall perpendicular to the one where she had found the sword. He held an open script in one hand.

"So what's your name?" he asked.

"Jordan. Jordan St. Clair."

"That's a beautiful name," said Jerry, smiling down at her.

"What's your middle name?" he asked.

The sword Jordan pressed against Jerry Martin's throat lacked the force to draw blood.

Despite her misgivings, Lisa Wong approached Jerry and his petite attacker. Tonya had talked her into it after Lisa initially refused.

"Look," Lisa had said, "I'm not a world-class assassin. I was in the one martial arts movie, but I'm not good with a sword.

"Plus I just want to make this abundantly clear. I'm Chinese, not Japanese and my parents are teachers. I am not a Kung Fu expert." With that she sighed and walked over to Jerry and Jordan.

Jerry's back was against a wall. He didn't dare move and risk the point of the blade cutting into his throat. He smiled at his co-star as she approached Jordan.

"So, Jordan," said Lisa. "You know who I am. Your friends have told me about you."

"But we skipped the part where you're a closet psycho," thought Jackie.

"This guy you have that sword aimed at is my friend," said Lisa.

"Whoever thought putting a real sword on the set was a good idea is going to be fired," said Jerry.

Lisa looked at him.

"We can talk about that after everyone gets their free lunch."

"Of course," said Jerry. "A free lunch for everyone. Wouldn't want to spoil that with an untimely fatal accident. Please continue saving my life. Didn't mean to interrupt."

"So to continue," said Lisa, "my friend here is British and he's unarmed. It would be dishonorable and cowardly to hurt him. He's like a talking bunny with a charming accent."

"It's not like there's a shortage of British people," said Jordan.

"True, but if you kill him, we might have to hire a Canadian."

"I like their bacon," said Jordan.

"Who doesn't?" said Jerry.

Jordan replaced the sword in its sheath, leaned the weapon against the wall where she had found it, sighed, and headed for the set's exit. Jackie and Tonya followed, avoiding eye contact with everyone else on the set.

"Can we talk about this thing you have with your middle name?" Jackie asked.

The three of them had returned to the Project Support offices in silence. Jordan sat behind her desk, her back toward her coworkers seated in front of her desk.

"No," said Jordan, bringing up a program on her computer that allowed her to see live feeds from security cameras outside their office building and inside the visitors area.

"I think maybe we should," said Tonya. "We don't hate you. We just want to understand."

"Shut the door," Jordan said.

"Sure," said Jackie.

"Now lock it," said Jordan.

"Really? How 'bout the main door?"

Jordan whirled around and looked at Jackie.

"Lock it NOW!"

"Yes, ma'am." Jackie heard the sound of the main door opening and she re-opened the office door just enough to see a very angry Linda Raymond enter their building's waiting area. The same Linda Raymond for whom they had bought tampons earlier.

Jordan ran full tilt into the door, slamming it shut and then locked the door.

"Get under my desk," said Jordan.

Linda Raymond started screaming from the other side of the locked door. It was hard to make out every word. The words "extra large tampons" were the loudest and clearest.

Jackie and Tonya looked at each other, ran behind the desk, and dove underneath.

"Wow. This is really kinda roomy down here. Especially for a tiny person's desk. What does she do with all this leg room?" asked Tonya.

"Shhh," Jackie said. "We don't need two crazy angry people."

Jordan appeared underneath her desk carrying her dart rifle.

"Good idea," whispered Jackie.

Jordan sat on the floor.

"She'll be gone in a couple of minutes. I can lock the outside door from in here after she leaves, but I haven't installed the automated locking system on our individual office doors just yet," Jordan said.

The shouting stopped and the three women gathered around Jordan's computer monitor to check the outer office video feed.

Linda Raymond threw magazines all over the floor. As she exited the building, she picked up a hammer sitting on a table and smashed a photo hanging near the main door.

"My bad," said Tonya. "I really should have put that away."

"That's okay," Jordan said.

"Not a problem," said Jackie. "Do you think we can get Carrie Smith to autograph another photo for us?"

Jordan used her computer to lock the entrance to their building.

9

"Are you three ready to deal with another celebrity?" asked The Manager via the speaker on Jordan's phone.

"So soon?" mouthed Tonya. "Our wall has barely recovered."

"We can't say 'no'," Jackie mouthed back to her.

Jordan nodded.

"I think you'll like this assignment. You get to sit outside for one day ... the weather's going to be great."

"That's what I've heard, sir," said Jordan. Her coworkers nodded.

"Your job is to watch someone. You don't have to get too close to this person. All you have to do is watch him."

The Manager paused.

The three women exchanged looks.

"So what's the catch, sir?" Jackie asked.

"It's Alan Jacobs," The Manager said.

"You have to keep an eye on him while he's in and around his trailer. But you don't have to go on the soundstage or in the trailer."

Alan Jacobs.

"The guy who trashed and torched his trailer last year?" asked Jackie.

"Yep. That's the one. He has a one day shoot on a movie that's about to wrap. He insisted on his own trailer, so in order to get the vehicle on studio property, the studio had to promise our insurance company we would have him watched."

"How does he feel about that?" asked Jackie. Tonya nodded.

"Good question," she mouthed to Jackie.

"He doesn't know," said The Manager.

"Excuse me?" said Jackie.

"He doesn't know he's going to be watched?" Tonya said.

"That's correct. We'll provide you with magazines, canopied lawn chairs, refreshments, meals, snacks … you'll have full access to craft services. You'll have the full 'star' treatment just like the leads in the movie."

"We'll do it," Jordan said.

"Sounds great! Thanks for the trust, sir," said Jackie.

Jordan's index finger ended the phone call.

"I'll bring extra ammo," she said.

"Sounds like a plan," said Jackie. Tonya nodded in agreement again.

"So here he comes," Jackie said.

Coolers sat next to each woman's chair and Jackie pulled a bottle of apple juice from hers as Alan Jacobs, his balding head shining in the sunlight surrounded by a horseshoe of hair, walked up to the door of his celebrity trailer.

The Project Support Team, all three sipping on beverages, concentrated on their drinks as they sat across the empty space separating the two rows of soundstages, Alan Jacob's indoor filming location being in the opposite row. Alan turned, taking note of the three women.

Each woman also had a small table beside her chair. On top of the tables sat an assortment of magazines. All three women turned to look through the closest stack of periodicals.

Unable to ignore his stare, the three women looked at him. Jacobs sighed, shook his head and entered his trailer.

"No smoke yet," said Jackie.

"Was that a bulge in his pants pocket? Do you think he has a lighter?" asked Tonya.

"No, I don't think there was a bulge. Just baggy pants," said Jordan.

"Nuts, anyone?" asked Jackie, holding an opened can in the direction of her coworkers.

"Do they have M&M's in them?" said Tonya.

"They wouldn't be fit for celebrities like us if they didn't," said Jackie. Jordan and Tonya each took a handful.

Thirty minutes later, as Alan Jacobs exited his trailer, no noise or smoke plumes followed his exit.

"No smoke is a good sign," Tonya observed.

"It's an omen," said Jackie, rummaging through Jordan's pile of magazines and picking out one to her liking. "May I borrow this, Ms. St. Clair?"

"Of course, Ms. Faraday."

A group of clowns walked between the rows of soundstages.

"Anyone we know?" asked Tonya. It was hard to tell with the makeup and costumes.

Jordan stood up and walked toward the group of performers as they looked over at the three women.

"Just keep walking," Jordan said and the suddenly nervous clowns left the area with a noticeable amount of haste.

Jackie rejoined her two coworkers and was about to sit down when Jordan caught her eye.

Jordan held up her right index finger. Jordan looked over at Tonya and then back at Jackie.

Jordan added her middle finger to her gesture.

Jackie looked at Tonya, hoping for an explanation.

"Number 1 or Number 2?" asked Jordan.

Jackie continued to look confused. Tonya made an effort to explain.

"Did you go pee, or did you go poo?" asked Tonya.

Jackie sighed, shook her head and sat down.

"You two are so sick," said Jackie.

"It's a game we're playing," said Tonya. "We call it, 'P-V-P'. Pee versus poo."

"So?" asked Jordan.

Jackie shook her head, refusing to make eye contact with either Jordan or Tonya. She sighed.

"Both," said Jackie, opening up a magazine.

Jordan waved her hands palms down in a crisscross pattern.

"It's a wash," she said. "Give me back my money."

Tonya handed currency to her.

"It's just a game. Something to kill the time," said Tonya.

Tonya and Jackie noticed Jordan looking elsewhere. They turned to see Alan Jacobs walking toward his trailer.

The three women locked eyes with him.

Seconds passed by.

Alan finally broke off the staring contest and entered his trailer.

Jordan held up her fingers again in the same pattern, first the index finger followed by an accompanying middle finger, and jerked her head once toward Alan Jacob's trailer.

"It'll cost you to find out," said Jackie. "I'm just here to watch him. If I don't see smoke and I don't smell smoke, I'm staying right here."

"Don't you wonder what he does in there?" Tonya asked.

"I'm not walking over there to find out," said Jackie and Jordan and Tonya laughed.

The three women noticed a group of chorus line dancers walking past their position. The dancers wore hose, their backs bare, and the rest of their strutting bodies were encased in tight, sparkling costumes.

"Wow," said Tonya. "Those girls are in such great shape. I need to go to the gym."

Jordan and Jackie looked at her. Tonya saw their looks.

"More often. I need to go to the gym more often. I usually exercise at home. I have a DVD. It's yoga. I'll show it to you next time you come over."

"Not all of them are girls," said Jordan, turning her attention to her magazine.

Jackie and Tonya looked at each other.

As Alan Jacobs made another trip to his trailer, he ignored the Project Support Team just as he had when he last exited his trailer. After he entered, he gave the door a hearty slam.

"Just when I thought he was going to be so cool about the whole thing," said Jackie.

"Very disappointing," said Tonya.

"Yep," said Jordan.

"Wanna take a break?" asked Tonya of Jordan.

"Sure."

When they returned, Jackie was grinning.

"Okay, so if I guess right, the two of you have to pay me."

Tonya looked at Jordan who nodded.

"Deal," said Tonya.

"Both," said Jackie. "You've been hitting craft services all day long and drinking water like a guy who just crawled out of the desert."

"Wrong, Kimosabe," said Jordan, taking her chair as Tonya did the same.

"Really? How can you do that? Are you both constipated?" asked Jackie.

"Nah, we saw Jacobs leave the set for a little stroll with some bigwigs and we snuck in a break while you went to craft services," said Tonya.

"Ah, man," Jackie said, shaking her head.

"Better luck next time, Sport," said Jordan.

"You know … that's cheating," said Jackie.

"You're not going to let it go are you?" Jordan said.

"Here he comes," said Tonya.

Alan Jacobs stopped several feet from his trailer door, turning to face the women.

They met his stare.

Jacobs seemed to grind his teeth and his face became a piece of malevolent stone.

He growled and walked toward the three women. Jackie and Tonya gripped the armrests of their chairs.

Jordan stood up and took off her jacket, exposing the gun on her hip. She laid her jacket on the insulated cooler next to her chair.

She returned to her chair; Jacobs changed direction and rushed to his trailer. The door closed quietly this time.

Jackie and Tonya grinned.

"That was so cool," said Tonya. "Can I hold your gun?"

"No, but you can touch it while it's in the holster," Jordan said. She stood up and walked over next to Tonya's chair. "By the way, never ask to touch a cop's gun. They won't let you and they don't like it when you ask."

"It's better than nothing," said Tonya. Jackie smiled.

A group of six men wearing multi-colored headdresses and orange Tibetan Lama robes with layered red and yellow undergarments came into view.

"Lamas," whispered Tonya.

"Wait till they get close," said Jackie.

Jordan looked over at the group, smiled and returned her attention to her book.

Jackie and Tonya stood and approached the group, keeping a respectful distance. As the men came opposite their surveillance position, Jackie and Tonya bowed at the waist.

Jordan stayed in her chair, but looked up to watch.

"We're not real monks," said one of the men.

"I grew up in Barstow," said another in the group and the others laughed.

Tonya and Jackie walked back to their chairs red-faced.

"Psyche," said Jordan. "They're wearing running shoes, not traditional footwear."

"How would you know?" Jackie asked.

"I've seen Tibetan Lama's in parades. Plus I've been to Tibet. And their English was very good. I could hear them talking as they got close to us. Their accents are American."

"What's Tibet like?" asked Tonya.

"Hilly. Kinda. Some nice shiny buildings. I was in a city mostly when I went."

"What are the people like?" asked Tonya.

"Couldn't really say. The ones at the hotel were nice enough. I wasn't there for very long."

Alan Jacobs exited the soundstage with three men and two women. The five were dressed in what looked like very expensive business attire.

"Great job!" said one man and the other four people nodded enthusiastically and smiled.

"Can we count on you for the sequel?" asked one of the women.

The mouths of all three Project Support Team members dropped open.

Two chorus line dancers appeared near Jacobs' soundstage, walking in a direction opposite the one they had last been seen traveling. Alan Jacobs took the opportunity to leer at the dancers.

"Those are girls, right?" Tonya asked.

"No, they are not," said Jordan.

Tonya and Jackie smiled.

10

"Hey, Jordan!"

"Yeah, Manny?"

"You got a call."

"Okay. Turn off the juice up there."

Jordan watched the welding equipment in her hand go dark. She let the darkness surround her for a moment as she rocked back and forth in the ocean currents. She lifted the welding screen on her diving helmet.

"Hello?" a familiar voice said.

"Go for St. Clair," said Jordan.

"Are you in the middle of something?" asked Tonya. "You sound far away."

"Kinda," said Jordan.

She made herself comfortable atop the nuclear submarine on which she was doing a patch job. It was barely more than a deep gouge, but the pay was really good.

"I can use a break," Jordan said.

"You sure? I can call back if you want."

Jordan looked up, seeing her hoses for air and welding disappear into the underside of the ocean's surface.

"Nah, I'm good. What's up?"

"It's about a guy I went out with," said Tonya.

"Have you known him long?"

"No, just a little while. We have mutual friends."

"Well, first off, it takes about six months to get to know someone," said Jordan.

"I haven't known you for much longer than that and I feel like I don't really know you," Tonya said. "Your voice sounds funny. Are you okay?"

"Yeah, I'm just working on something."

Jordan patted the top of the submarine.

"I have some weird hobbies. I have to wear protective gear sometimes. So did you read the books I gave you on body language and interrogation techniques?"

"Not all the way. I kinda skimmed. Sorry."

"Oh, that's okay. It's kind of dry stuff. Let's go over the basics. Eye movement and vocal pitch."

Jordan scooted backwards and to the side so she could lean against the submarine's conning tower while remaining seated.

Another couple of hours and the job would be over. A few hours after that, she would be traveling with her surface support team to a small coastal town. Via a small airstrip's rented plane, she would start working her way up the ladder of civilization and technology until she landed in L.A. on a large jet full of tourists and businesspeople late Sunday night.

Her thoughts started to drown out Tonya's narrative until Jordan remembered something.

"Oh. Sorry to interrupt. I'll be in late on Monday. After lunch."

"That's okay. I interrupted you and whatever you're doing." said Tonya. "You do that pretty often, come in late on Mondays, or don't come in at all."

"Yeah. Management's okay with it," said Jordan.

"Good. So where was I?" asked Tonya.

"You were talking about his last ex being kinda creepy."

"Oh, yeah."

Jordan sighed quietly and closed her eyes as she tried to concentrate on Tonya's story, but couldn't help smiling as she pictured herself falling asleep in her L.A. twin bed.

11

"I think that's deep enough," said Tonya, laying the soil auger on the ground.

"You think?" asked Jackie.

"Yep. According to the instructions, we have enough little holes spread out just right to blow one giant hole in Steven Spielberg's lawn right where he wants his new pool."

"It's a monument to efficiency," said Jackie.

Tonya looked at her.

"Well, sure. The hole should move the project ahead by at least a couple of days."

Jackie looked behind them at Jordan who stood about thirty yards away, avoiding any dirt plumes.

"Look okay to you?" Jackie asked.

"You two are the brains of this operation," said Jordan. "I'm more of a C-4 gal. I'll go get the dynamite out of the van."

Jordan walked the length of two football fields to reach the minivan. She removed two large buckets from inside the Project Support vehicle.

In one bucket was the dynamite. In the other, a wireless detonator sitting on top of several blasting caps. The necessary wiring had already been moved to the excavation site.

Jordan jumped a little when she heard footsteps behind her.

She turned and Steven Spielberg held out his hand.

"Hey! How's it going?" he asked.

His wife, Kate Capshaw, stood nearby.

Jordan put down the buckets and shook his hand.

"We haven't seen you around here in a while," said Kate.

"I've been busy. I'll be here for the party in a couple of weeks."

"We look forward to seeing you there," said Mrs. Spielberg.

Mr. Spielberg looked across the estate at Jackie and Tonya examining the holes in the ground. Both women simultaneously noticed someone was looking at them and who that someone was. Jackie and Tonya adjusted their hard hats and fluorescent vests in the distance.

"How's the pool project going?" asked Steven.

"Swimmingly," said Jordan and the three of them laughed. Jackie and Tonya, seeing and hearing the laughter just barely, looked at the Spielbergs and then at each other.

"It looks good to me, but those two are in charge," Jordan said, pointing to her coworkers. "I'm just the muscle." Steven and Kate laughed.

"Need some help?" asked Mr. Spielberg. Kate Capshaw grabbed her husband by the arm.

"Let the experts handle it," she said.

"It probably would be best if you stayed here," said Jordan.

"We'll stay right here," said Kate.

"I just wanted to help."

"Like I would ever let you near dynamite. You just stay right here with me and supervise."

Jordan picked up the buckets and returned to her coworkers.

"Did they say anything about us?" asked Jackie.

"Do they think we're doing a good job?" asked Tonya.

"They have faith in you and they think everything looks great," Jordan said.

Jackie and Tonya gave each other a nod and a smile.

Some tamping of dynamite sticks and wire-connecting followed. Jordan did a battery check on the wireless detonator.

Jackie stepped back and admired their handiwork.

"This is going to work. We're good here, right?"

Tonya looked through her notes and reviewed the final layout of the high explosives.

She put her notebook in a pocket adorning her fluorescent vest.

"We followed Terry's instructions. We should be ready to light this lawn up!" she said.

"Terry. Terry the Special Effects department guy?" asked Jackie.

"Yep."

"Terry the Special Effects guy you broke up with?"

"We agreed it was mutual. It was time for us both to move on."

As Jackie and Tonya discussed the side effects of breakups, Jordan slipped away at a brisk pace that turned into a full run as she headed toward the minivan.

Jordan looked at the Spielbergs as she checked her pockets to make sure she had the key fob.

"Is there a problem?" Kate asked.

"Not yet," said Jordan.

The Spielbergs looked at each other and jumped in the passenger seats behind the driver's position. Jordan put the van in reverse and backed up the driveway to the main house and then down another driveway that took the three of them far away from the demolition project.

While the minivan and its occupants moved to a safe position, Jackie and Tonya stepped backwards from the explosives planted in the yard.

Jackie and Tonya looked over their shoulders, barely able to make out the minivan.

"Should we have backed up farther?" Jackie said.

"Terry said about a hundred yards should be good."

"Terry said," repeated Jackie and sighed.

"Okay, good ol' Terry. We can trust him."

"Put on your safety glasses," Tonya said.

"Oh, yeah. Thanks.

"Shouldn't the detonator look like that thing in the cartoons?"

"This is the 21st Century. There's probably a phone app we could use if we just knew where to look," said Tonya.

"Let's be thankful someone else didn't find it while we're standing so close," said Jackie.

"Amen to that. Fire in the hole!" said Tonya as she flicked two switches on the handheld detonator.

The sun was obscured for a moment. Then all the dirt in the world seemed headed directly for Jackie and Tonya.

After the dirt had fallen back from whence it came, the only parts of Jackie and Tonya's bodies still clean were the parts covered by their hard hats and safety glasses.

"Think you used enough dynamite there, Butch?" asked Jackie.

Tonya grinned.

"I don't know. Let's go take a look at the hole."

Jackie and Tonya examined their handiwork. Jordan and the Spielbergs joined them to peer down at the smoldering lawn crater.

Kate Capshaw turned toward another part of the estate.

"You know … I think I'd like the new pool over there," she said.

"Only don't use dynamite this time. It scares the horses."

With that Mrs. Spielberg turned and walked toward the main house.

Mr. Spielberg looked at the back of his wife's head for a moment and then at Jordan.

"Can you put all the dirt back and call a gardener?"

"Mmmm … we don't do that kind of work," said Jordan.

"Just paperwork …" said Tonya.

"… errand running …" said Jackie.

"And high explosive demolition," finished Jordan.

Steven Spielberg smiled.

"That's okay. I know a couple of guys who can handle this sort of thing. My assistant will give them a call."

J.J. Abrams sighed and adjusted his safety glasses as he sat in the enclosed driver's seat of the mini front loader. He turned to George Lucas who stood several feet away.

George made a gesture toward the pile of dirt directly in front of the machine, urging J.J. to shove more dirt into the previously planned pool site.

"Did Steven ever say why he got the sudden urge to blow a hole in his lawn?" asked J.J.

"Nope. I'm just in charge of the clipboard," George said, waving his portable writing surface in the air. "Don't forget your hard hat."

J.J. sighed again and reached down at his feet for his safety headwear.

"Don't forget your safety glasses," J.J. said.

"Oh, yeah. Thanks!"

J.J. started the compact front loader's engine, adjusted the lever next to the operator's seat and moved the machine forward pushing dirt into the crater made by the now absent Project Support Team.

12

"It's not very glamorous back here," said Jackie, looking around the sci-fi convention backstage hallway.

"There are stars participating in panels out front," Jordan said. "That's the glamorous part."

"Back here it's just concrete floors, concrete walls, concrete everything," said Tonya. "Oh, and there's the rolling food racks and of course these wonderful silver refrigerators." She ended her observation by reaching for a nearby appliance's door.

"Don't touch that," Jordan said.

Jackie walked toward what looked like a curtained alcove.

"What's in here?" she asked.

Jordan put her hand on Jackie's arm. As she spoke, Jordan did so in a whisper.

"Step away from there," she said.

"Those shorter curtains are there to mark a temporary green room slash makeup area. There are likely some very large, highly trained bodyguards in there, guarding celebrities or their crap."

"How did we get this gig anyway?" asked Jackie. "Some rich chick loses her purse and we're supposed to find it among thousands of fans?"

"We were given the assignment because she's a powerful rich chick," said Jordan.

"It's a bucket bag made out of snakeskin. Granted you have to sneak those in from out of state, but it ought to stand out," said Tonya as the three continued their search.

"It doesn't stand out because there are people at the convention who brought snakes and there are people who are dressed as snakes," Jordan said.

"I guess running into some big scary guys would be pretty rough since Security took your gun away," said Jackie.

"They only took the gun I wanted them to take," Jordan said, opening her coat to reveal the gun on her hip.

"You had another gun?" Tonya asked.

"Or maybe someone returned my gun or gave me another one," said Jordan.

Jackie thought back to when they had walked through the main exhibition hall. People had bumped into Jordan on multiple occasions. Jordan seemed to take it in stride from Jackie's viewpoint. She had assumed Jordan was used to collisions and near misses because Jordan was so petite. Apologies were issued by the offenders and Jordan had responded with a smile.

Snapping back to current events, Jackie saw a much thicker more expensive set of curtains on one side of the hallway. The curtains didn't seem to mark merely another alcove.

"So what's behind these?" asked Jackie.

Before Jordan could stop her, Jackie walked through an opening in the fabric wall.

Tonya eagerly followed.

Jordan was the last member of the Project Support Team to push through the heavy fabric and step onto the stage. Thousands of eyes in the darkened presentation hall focused on the three newcomers. The people seated at the well-lit panel table also turned and stared at the three women.

Jackie and Tonya moved quickly again, but not toward an opening in the curtains. They moved in a blur toward two celebrities seated at the table.

Jackie wrapped her arms around Chris Evans from behind. The focal of Tonya's physical affections was Chris Hemsworth seated next to Mr. Evans.

Jordan moved forward and began gently pulling Jackie and Tonya away from the startled but amused celebrities.

"We're here to protect The Talent, ladies, not choke them to death," said Jordan as she shoved her barely cooperative coworkers toward the opening in the curtains through which they had entered.

Robert Downey, Jr., seeing Jordan look his way, smiled, pointed an imaginary finger pistol at Jordan and winked.

"I loved the dress you wore to the party last weekend," Gwyneth Paltrow said, leaning back in her chair so she could see behind Mr. Downey's head. She seemed unaffected by the sudden intrusion of two affectionate strangers.

"Oh, that," said Jordan. "It was just something I bought off the rack."

"Still, you looked nice," said Gwyneth.

"Thank you."

Jordan turned and exited through the curtain opening.

"You know them?" asked Tonya.

"Who are you?" asked Jackie.

"I'm not sure anymore," Jordan said.

She walked around her coworkers to continue the search for the missing snakeskin bucket bag.

13

(Jordan's World: Pilot)

Jordan sighed.

She pushed the button on the recording studio control room's intercom mic.

"Say ..."

She looked over at the sound board operator.

"I don't remember his name either," Roy said and he turned back to the mixing switches.

She spoke into the microphone.

"Roy is ready to call it a day," Jordan said to the musician in the recording studio's live room. "Why don't we try this again next weekend?"

The musician took off his headphones and departed.

"He's a friend of my cousin," said Roy in response to the look Jordan gave him.

"He's actually really good," said Jordan. "It's just a low energy day. We'll try it again another time.

"I have a couple of friends who might want come in and just fool around. They could say they made a professional recording. You mind hanging around for a little while? You're paid up for the next hour, right?"

Roy smiled.

"I don't have to be anywhere. Send 'em in whenever you're ready. My laundry can wait."

"Yeah, I kinda figured it might be laundry day when I saw you wearing that mint condition 70's Star Wars shirt."

"It's all that was left," Roy said.

"Not a problem," said Jordan and she gave him a quick hug and a kiss on the cheek.

"Seriously, Roy, thanks. I'm hoping the song will do well. All I have to do is get it out there to the masses."

"I like the hook."

"Thanks," said Jordan.

Roy repositioned his glasses and made more adjustments at the mixing console.

Jordan exited the control room and walked down the hallway to the studio lobby. Seated on the lobby's red vinyl sectional couch were Christian Bale and Sir Michael Caine.

"Hey, guys!" Jordan said.

"Jordan!" said Christian. He and Michael stood up and took turns bending down to hug her.

"Wonderful to see you!" said Michael.

"Likewise!" she said. "I know you two are very busy, so I'll get right to it."

"Sure," Michael said. "Always ready to participate in one of your little games."

"Here's the phone," said Jordan, handing a cell phone to Christian. "Just press the call button and say the words on this piece of paper. I have the phone set to use the speaker."

All three of them heard Tonya's voice.

"Hello?"

"Alfred! I've been poisoned! Hurry! I need the antidote!" Christian shouted into the phone.

He ended the call and handed the phone back to Jordan. He and Michael Caine snickered.

"You're sure your friends won't mind? Won't they know it's your phone?" asked Michael.

Jordan punched in Jackie's phone number.

"No, it's a special phone. It's untraceable," said Jordan.

Jordan handed the phone to Sir Michael as Jackie's phone rang.

"Hello," said Jackie.

"Master Bruce! Hang on! I have the antidote! I'll be right there! You have to hang on!"

Jordan took the phone back and ended the call.

"You are so twisted," said Christian.

"It's good clean fun, though," Michael said.

Jordan hugged them both again.

"Speaking of clean fun. I have to leave, but I have an hour of studio time left if you'd like to lay down a track or two."

"Up for a bit of karaoke?" said Michael.

"'Don't Go Breaking My Heart'?" Christian asked.

"Let's give it a go. After you, Master Bruce."

They both laughed as they turned toward the recording studio. Christian Bale paused and spoke to Jordan.

"Where are you off to?" he asked as Jordan moved toward the hallway leading to the building's exit.

She turned and smiled.

"I gotta go see a man about a tiger."

"You want me to take you here?" asked the private jet's pilot, looking at a map and the coordinates Jordan had given him.

"Yes," she said.

Dressed in olive drab clothing, she stood just behind the pilot and copilot seats as the two men prepared for takeoff. Two duffle bags were tucked under separate but adjacent empty seats behind her in the main cabin.

"You and your friend better have some great survival skills," the pilot said.

"We do. But his are better. He was born to survive."

The pilot nodded. The copilot squeezed out of his seat to close the jet's outer door and Jordan took a seat across the aisle from the duffle bags.

The copilot returned to his seat and the plane began to taxi. Jordan spoke out loud in the empty airplane cabin.

"Just a few hours, my friend.

"See you soon, J.T."

14

(JW: Pilot cont'd)

To reach J.T. faster, Jordan hired a single engine plane from which to parachute. The private jet had enabled her to reach a small city in the same region as her final destination, but from there the runways located closer to the jungle were dirt. Of course, within the jungle there were no runways. She would have to parachute in and walk out, but she had slept during part of her journey and, though petite at first glance, she was not just skin and bones. She was muscle, skin, and bones.

As she floated down, she took a quick bearing from a radio receiver. She only needed to get close. They always found each other once they were near one another.

Once on the ground, she didn't try to move quietly through the underbrush and trees. The more noise the sooner J.T. would find her.

Jordan took a sip of water from a water bottle, noting a familiar paw print on the ground. She smiled, bent to take a second look and then stood up.

There he was a short distance away peering out from between the trees.

She called him J.T., but only J.T. knew his real name.

The tiger regarding her from the group of trees wore a heavy duty tracking collar around his neck. The piece of metal dangling from the bottom glinted in the sun as he walked out from the tree line toward her.

"J.T.!" she said and ran to the tiger loping toward her. She hugged him around his neck and he rubbed his head gently against hers.

Jordan led him back to the spot where she had left her duffle bags and an insulated satchel. J.T. sniffed the satchel.

"Yes, I have something for you to eat. You think I would show up without a present?"

She walked with him to a nearby shady tree grove where the trees were large and numerous enough to hide them but their position also gave her line of sight to watch for danger.

As J.T. ate his meat, Jordan checked the pistols and knives she carried. She knew everything was as it should be, but you didn't get a lot of second chances in the kinds of places where J.T. lived. After checking her weapons, she put on a pair of leather fingerless gloves.

When J.T. had finished his meal, she made two fists as the tiger laid back so she could use her knuckles to massage his sides and chest. Whenever she leaned in close to his head, he would lick her face each time.

"I love you, too," she said as J.T. rolled onto his side. She laid down, using his body as a pillow. She hummed a few bars from an Elvis song, grew quiet, and stared up at the sky for a few minutes before speaking.

"I hope you've been well. I've been coping as well as I can. I've been looking for ways to increase my cash flow. As usual. Most are working out pretty well.

"I have a couple of new friends. You'd like them.

"I need friends. They're not like family just yet, the new ones, but maybe someday."

She reached up and gently rubbed his side.

"It's a tough world out there. It's a dog eat dog world. And sometimes, if no one is watching, it's a tiger eat dog world."

J.T. growled softly.

Jordan looked up at the sky as J.T. began to doze off from the sedative she had put in the meat. She closed her eyes as she recalled the first time she had met her tiger friend.

Jordan lay in the brush taking pictures of some very evil men. The telescopic lens guaranteed she didn't have to get close to their outdoor meeting.

It was very unusual to see tigers in that part of the world, but when one tiger crossed the path of another one it usually ended violently. Tigers are very territorial.

Jordan heard the two animals growling from several yards to her left. She could see a fight was coming and she flattened herself to the ground as she took her last pictures of the men. Someone was probably going to end up dead from that event as well.

She liked reconnaissance work.

No bloodshed, no mess to clean up, not that she minded cleaning up other people's messes.

The killing jobs always bothered her. International gun laws aside, terminating someone's life required a lot of work to get in close and then get out fast. She preferred stealth. The kills were always righteous, justified. It was the guilt and the strange energy she felt when someone's life suddenly ended that was uncomfortable.

Killing people did pay well.

Photography jobs were much more to her liking. You get some exercise, some travel, you gather evidence and you're gone. Easy peasy.

The two tigers' eventual physical conflict would certainly attract attention from even a distance as far away as the clandestine meeting.

As the two animals closed, one of them looked her way. Their eyes met.

Jordan felt her eyebrows tingle.

The other tiger chose to make the most of the moment and leaped at his distracted opponent's neck.

Jordan felt remorse and rage at the same time.

As the tigers' bodies met, she was already in midair aiming for the attacker's back. She stabbed him three times to give her new friend a fighting chance.

She jumped clear of the dust and noise, using the additional momentum gained from being flung from the tiger's back. Her tiny body soared through the air. Her flight path was timed to take her in the direction of her camera and other equipment. She crawled along the ground as the group of men took notice of the animals' battle. The men laughed and immediately began making wagers as to the outcome.

The wounded attacker broke off from the fight and disappeared into the trees to Jordan's right; no doubt to lick his wounds.

Jordan grabbed her things and crawled passed the tree line behind her original position. The battle's victor followed a course parallel to hers without looking her way. Wicked men swapped currency far away.

Once she reached the trees, Jordan stood up and began moving fast. The tiger kept pace with her until the men were far behind them. The animal changed course to move near her.

Their faces grew close as they ran through the jungle and both hopped over roots, weaving through the trees. Realizing she might have a new friend, Jordan gradually slowed to a stop and looked into the tiger's eyes that were two feet from her own. Reaching into one of her duffle bags she pulled out a solar powered radio tracking collar and put it around his neck. She rubbed his face with her hands and the tiger gave her face a single lick to formally acknowledge their relationship.

After his nap, Jordan and J.T. walked until they came within sight of human civilization. She didn't dare take him any closer. Tiger body parts were worth a lot of money.

"I know your teeth and butt hurt.

"But I am your dentist and your doctor and you needed shots. Your heart and lungs will thank me later."

J.T. moved closer to her and he nuzzled her face as she ran her hand down his neck.

"I have a job coming up soon where I can use your help. You don't have to eat anyone. I just need some backup.

"There's good food, air travel, and a lot of adventure. You get to see and smell new places."

She stopped, took his head in her hands and looked into his eyes.

"Sound good?"

He licked her face.

She hugged him for a few seconds.

She let go of him, backing away toward civilization.

"Be well my friend. I love you."

Her eyes began to water as she turned toward the distant gathering of buildings. She heard grass part behind her as J.T. returned to his Wild and the cover of trees and tall thick grass.

More air travel and a Monday off in L.A. awaited her.

15

(JW: The Crossover)

Jordan walked down the front steps of the three story apartment building carrying a large area rug over her shoulder. It was dark out and the occupants of the apartments just above and below street level had their curtains closed.

If the tenants' curtains had been open, the occupants might have spotted the body-shaped bulge in the carpet.

Jordan whistled softly as she walked toward the borrowed Project Support minivan.

"Mr. Taylor, you'd be a lot easier to carry if your butt wasn't so big," she said to the rug. "Of course, if you had been more careful about choosing your friends, I wouldn't be carrying you around Venice late at night. And I wouldn't have had to clean up that awful mess in your old apartment."

She pushed a button on the minivan key fob and the side doors slid open.

"Of course I didn't make the mess, but the mess helps pay my bills, so I forgive you."

She gave the bulge a couple of pats.

"And you won't be making anymore poor social choices ever again."

She managed to flop and shove the rug and its contents into the minivan.

Through the minivan's opposite opened door, she saw Jackie and Tonya sitting on a park bench sipping frozen beverages.

Jordan used the key fob to close the doors and walked to the back of the vehicle to chat with her coworkers who stood and approached her.

"Buenos nachos," said Jordan.

"Hey," said Jackie.

"Hi!" Tonya said.

"We were taking a walk and saw the van," said Jackie.

"We walked over and checked out the plates," said Tonya.

"Sure enough. Our van," Jackie said.

"We stood around for a while and then we decided to sit down and see if anyone we knew showed up," said Tonya.

"And here you are!" said Jackie. Tonya smiled and nodded.

"So do you do housekeeping on the weekends?" asked Jackie.

Before Jordan could reply, Tonya spoke.

"Is that why you miss work on Mondays sometimes?"

"You must be really tired," Jackie said.

"You could call it housekeeping," said Jordan.

Jackie and Tonya looked at each other.

"We could use some extra money, right?" Jackie asked Tonya.

"Sure. You bet," said Tonya. "If it would help you out. But not all the time. Just part-time, once in a while. Casual part-time work."

"Exactly," said Jackie.

"Sure," said Jordan. "I have some manual labor gigs and some clerical-type work available. If you're interested."

"That last kind sounds good," said Tonya. Jackie nodded.

"We wouldn't have to wear uniforms would we?" Jackie asked.

"Just once in a while. But it would all be very casual," said Jordan. "And there might be travel. And three day weekends, too."

"Great!" Jackie said.

"Perfect," said Tonya.

"Well, I have to run. That carpet isn't going to clean itself.

"I'll give you my home address later. We can meet up sometime soon so we can discuss the details.

"And give you your uniforms."

"Great!" Jackie said and Tonya nodded.

Jordan climbed into the minivan's driver seat and drove away before Jackie and Tonya had the chance to examine the minivan's cargo.

"How do you like your outfits?" asked Jordan.

"They're pajamas," Jackie said.

"With a logo on the blouse pocket," said Tonya.

"'JSC-HQ'," she read out loud.

"It's a division of Jordan St. Clair Enterprises," said Jordan.

Jackie looked at Jordan.

"You have a really nice house," Tonya said as she looked around the first floor.

Jordan smiled.

"I like living among regular middle class people," she said.

"Or what passes for 'regular' in Venice," Jackie said.

"And you have a nice rec center across the street," said Tonya.

"The house is an architectural school graduation project. An extraordinary house amongst ordinary people and their ordinary lives. I like ordinary. I like simple."

"So what's up with making us wear slippers?" asked Jackie.

"Well, they're gifts but can serve other purposes. I bought you bear claw slippers because you like to jump in feet first to reach a goal and your shoes warn people not to mess with you. Tonya is wearing bunny slippers as a distraction."

Jordan walked over to a nearby closet and returned with an aluminum bat. She handed the bat to Tonya.

"While they're staring at the bunnies you smack them with that.

"Let me show you where you'll be working. Sometimes."

Jackie and Tonya looked at each other and followed Jordan to an upstairs bedroom. Tonya brought her bat.

Inside the room were large computer monitors and a metal cabinet with lots of black computer-looking boxes adorned with blinking lights.

"That hum you're hearing is the cooling fans inside the server rack," said Jordan. "Most of that equipment is used for masking network traffic from any curious parties."

"Who would be curious about what you do with computers?" Jackie asked.

Jordan smiled.

"You'd be surprised. With this equipment and this special phone, you'll be able to monitor my movements via satellite and let me know if things are safe."

"Safe to do what?" asked Jackie.

"Anything. Walk into a building, walk out of a building. If I'm supposed to meet one person, you make sure there aren't six hiding in the bushes nearby.

"I like to use this monitor for visual feeds and this other one for infrared, heat signatures, and electromagnetic radiation type data."

"We have to work at night?" Tonya asked.

"No, not necessarily, but I often do. It might be dark where I'm at and still daytime here in California.

"I really appreciate you two helping me out. I'll be telling you more as we go along."

Jordan picked up two envelopes lying on a nearby table.

"Take this for now. A little something for your trouble. I really do hope you'll be comfortable working in my home and with the travel arrangements I make for us."

Jackie and Tonya looked inside their envelopes.

"Good enough for a couple hours work?"

"Very good enough," said Jackie.

"Oh yeah," Tonya said.

"Good. We'll be traveling next weekend. I've made arrangements for you to visit a doctor to be immunized. We'll be traveling overseas."

Jordan paused to let her coworkers chat among themselves and then resumed.

"We'll technically be working at night according to Pacific Time. I'll provide all the clothing and equipment.

"Except for undies."

"Thank goodness for that," said Jackie. Tonya snickered.

As Jackie and Tonya left Jordan's house, Tonya turned to Jordan and said, "I know who you are."

Jordan looked Tonya in the eye.

"You do?"

"Yes, you're our boss. Our weekend boss," Tonya said.

"I'm just a friend who appreciates your help. And gives you money," said Jordan.

"We appreciate that. And we're glad to help," said Jackie. "And the extra work … it'll be a bonding experience."

"Just a part-time bonding experience," said Jordan. "I wouldn't want you to get tired of me."

"Not a chance," said Tonya. She bent over to hug Jordan. Jackie did likewise after Tonya straightened and backed away.

"See you on Monday," said Tonya.

"See you," Jordan said.

Jordan closed the front door. She leaned back against the door and sighed.

"I forgot to ask if they have any experience with firearms," she said to her empty house.

"Or if they're allergic to tigers."

16

(JW: Recon)

"I swear … that thing is going to eat me," said Tonya.

J.T. licked his paws, ignoring the nervous Tonya standing several feet from him. He sat in a soft patch of grass inside the tree line while Jackie and Tonya watched Jordan crawl through much taller grass toward a compound surrounded by a ten foot fence. An area nearly one hundred yards deep with patches of grass and dirt formed a barrier between the fence and the main house. Timing meant everything with regard to achieving Jordan's goal.

"Don't say it so loudly," Jackie said as she scanned the area through binoculars. "You don't want to give him any ideas."

Tonya sighed.

"He didn't seem to mind all the traveling. He looks tame."

"Yep," said Jackie without turning around.

"The planes, the sneaky jeep ride. The trail up the mountain to avoid the cliff. He took it all really well.

"I won't need to go to Pilates for a month."

"I hear ya," said Jackie.

"Does your camo makeup make your face itch? I'll never get used to this stuff."

"Yes. My face itches. A little."

"I like the clothes. They're all camouflage colored but they're soft like the ninja pajamas. And I like all the pockets. Jordan always makes sure we have plenty of pockets."

J.T. stopped cleaning himself and stared at Tonya. She moved a little closer to Jackie.

"Of course after Jordan gets us up here, she goes sneaking off through the grass to cut her way into the Bad Guys' jungle lair.

"What was the name of that funny looking outfit that makes her look like a little walking bush?"

"A ghillie suit," said Jackie.

"Yeah, right. I looked it up online while we still had access to the Web. Snipers wear those things."

Tonya looked over at J.T.

"He blends in, too. I can see how Jordan does it. The special suit, the makeup, being all sneaky and crawling around.

"How does he do it? Look at him. Parts of him are orange."

Jackie lowered the binoculars to look over at the tiger. J.T. stared in the direction in which Jordan had left.

"He's a tiger. That's what he does. It's his job to be sneaky. And eat things."

Jackie caught herself.

"But not us," she said.

"Right. But not us," said Tonya.

Jackie raised the binoculars again.

"I'm not worried," said Jackie.

"Why not?"

"I can run faster than you," Jackie said.

"Ha ha."

Jackie reached behind herself and grabbed Tonya's arm.

"She's in. The guards are on the other side of the house and she just cut her way in by making a little hole in the fence.

"She did it really fast."

"Do you think she's done this before?" Tonya asked.

Jordan entered the main house through an open window. She wondered what kind of bad guy put his computer near a window and then left the window open.

"Oh, well. It means I get out of here faster and get my money that much sooner," Jordan muttered to herself.

She pulled out two thumb drives from inside her clothing, one green and one red. She inserted the green one into the computer.

A logon window appeared and she entered a password. She removed the green thumb drive and inserted the red one.

She navigated through the computer's file system until she found the files she had been told to look for and copied them to the red thumb drive.

When the files had been copied, she removed the thumb drive, tucked it away, and locked the computer again.

She heard a noise behind her.

She turned.

A very large, sweaty man stood outside the open window glaring at her.

"Hand me the thumb drive," he said.

She reached inside her clothing.

Instead of the red thumb drive, she pulled out a snub nose .38 caliber revolver and shot him in the head. Just as he hit the ground, three more men entered the room where Jordan stood in her ghillie suit and makeup holding her pistol. Catching sight of the pistol, the men hesitated.

Jordan threw herself out the window, hit the ground and rolled to her feet.

"J.T.!" she yelled.

The men moved to the window. One spoke into a walkie-talkie while the other two drew their weapons. They took aim at Jordan as she ran toward the fence.

J.T. cleared the fence and his momentum carried him past Jordan and toward the men with the pistols. They slammed the window shut out of reflex.

J.T. whirled back in Jordan's direction, leaving a huge cloud of dust and grass in his wake. J.T. looked over his shoulder at the frightened men as Jordan mounted his back. She grabbed the hand grip on the chest harness he wore as he crouched. He was going full speed as he leaped over the fence.

"Holy crap! Here they come," Jackie said.

"Wait. Are those guys in the jeep headed this way?" asked Tonya.

"Who cares? Once they reach the trees they won't be able to drive the jeep any further."

"But they have guns. Won't they be able to shoot between the trees?"

Jackie looked at her.

"We should start running," said Jackie.

It was at that moment that J.T. and his passenger ran past them.

"Good idea!" said Tonya.

She and Jackie grabbed the nearby equipment bags and started running.

"I thought you said you could run faster than me!" said Tonya.

"Oh, shut up!"

Tonya laughed.

Somewhere behind them came the sound of multiple gun shots.

"I could really use a tiger right now," Jackie said as Jordan and J.T. disappeared over a small hill ahead of them.

"Really? I think I'd like an ostrich!"

"You'd look cute on an ostrich!"

"Thanks! I wish that hill was closer!"

"Hill … good!" said Jackie.

Tonya nodded.

"Cliff … bad," she said.

They arrived on the other side of the hill and looked over the edge of the cliff.

They reached into their equipment bags and put on rock climbing harnesses. They each pulled out a rope that extended to the base of the cliff after it was attached to the rock slab on which they stood. They were putting on gloves when a bullet hit the mound of dirt above them.

"This is a lot more fun than the rock climbing gym," said Tonya.

Jackie looked at her as they both pushed themselves backwards over the cliff.

"Nobody shoots at me when I'm at the gym!" she said.

As they rappelled down the mountain's sheer face, Jackie and Tonya noticed Jordan and J.T. finishing their descent with Jordan still atop J.T.'s back. Jordan removed their climbing gear and she and J.T. ran to a nearby jeep.

Jordan started the engine while J.T. grunted as he squeezed into the space behind the rear seat.

Jackie and Tonya reached the bottom of the cliff, disconnected themselves from their equipment, and ran toward the jeep.

"Shotgun!" yelled Jackie and laughed as she threw herself into the passenger seat beside Jordan. Tonya, too tired to complain, eased into the back seat in a position behind Jordan.

"J.T. likes you," said Jordan.

"How can you tell?" said Tonya.

"He's not eating you!"

Jordan shoved the jeep into gear and slammed on the accelerator. The three women and one tiger disappeared into the grass and trees before the men at the top of the cliff could figure out what had happened.

"Have a safe trip back to L.A." said Jordan.

"You, too. It won't be the same without your tiger," Jackie said.

Jordan smiled.

"Where are you going?" asked Tonya.

"I have to take J.T. home."

"Why is your plane so much bigger than ours?" Tonya asked.

"The pilots requested J.T. sit way in the back."

Jackie and Tonya laughed.

"I bet," said Tonya.

"Your plane is still a jet," Jordan said.

"I guess it will do," said Jackie.

"Tell J.T. we enjoyed working with him," said Tonya.

"Liar," said Jackie.

Jordan turned and walked toward her plane where J.T. sat curled up at the bottom of the boarding ramp.

After watching Jordan and J.T. walk up the ramp, Jackie and Tonya moved toward their smaller jet's entrance.

"I wonder why the bad guys didn't come after us?" said Tonya.

"Maybe after whatever happened in that house, they had to run for it."

"That makes sense."

The two women heard a noise and saw Jordan waving goodbye to them from the other plane's open door.

Jackie and Tonya did the same and entered the private jet. They planned to make the most of what was left of their first Jordan-orchestrated three day weekend.

17

(JW: Jordan St. Clair and the Shoe of Stolen Dreams)

The business park offices were stacked on top of each other in a U-shaped fashion so as to fit more square footage into a smaller area. The property rented to a mix of modest and upscale clientele; dentists, doctors, and law firms for example.

The business the woman was looking for did not fall into those categories.

She mounted the wide staircase built with one perpendicular turn and entered the shadows created by the overhanging second story roof. She passed a small startup software company with its blinds shut, walked passed a weight loss group's local HQ, and stopped in front of a door with the following inscription on a nearby window whose blinds were open:

ST. CLAIR INVESTIGATIONS

(A Division of JSC Enterprises)

The woman pushed the large unlocked door open and saw three desks to her left. Seeing no receptionist, she ventured farther into the office, the front door closing quietly behind her.

Jordan stepped out of an office in the back. The blinds that covered her office's narrow interior window were shut. The woman's attention was drawn to Jordan's slightly darkened glasses.

"Hello. Do you work here?"

"I'm the owner," said Jordan. "I'm sorry no one was out here to greet you."

She offered her hand to the visitor.

"My name is Jordan. And you are?"

"Amy Cedillo."

Jordan watched as the woman nervously spun the wedding ring on her left hand.

"Most of my operatives have the weekend off, Ms. Cedillo. May I get you something to drink?"

"I'm fine. I need to hire you and I don't like talking about the subject I need to tell you about. I just want to get this over with."

"I see. Come right in."

Jordan shut her office door as the woman sat down in a guest chair in front of Jordan's glass and steel desk.

"What can I help you with?" asked Jordan, easing into the chair behind her desk. "I can assure you we are very discreet."

"This is much nicer than I expected."

"Yes, we're not a shady gumshoe type of business. We use the latest in technology and use every resource we have at our disposal to help our clients."

Jordan paused.

"How may I be of assistance?"

"I need to talk to you about a murder."

"You don't seem like a killer and you don't look like the type of person that hangs out with an unsavory crowd. How'd you come to be involved with this matter?"

The woman could feel Jordan's undivided attention.

"It was my husband. He was murdered."

Jordan sat back.

"I'm very sorry for your loss. Would you like a tissue?"

"No, no thank you.

"To be honest, at this point I'm more angry than sad."

"Go on."

"I've been counting on the police to find answers, but nothing has happened. I'm okay so far as money is concerned. My parents left me some money. And my husband, Frank, had a sizable life insurance policy."

"I see," Jordan said.

"The police haven't helped though and a friend of mine, her husband, works for the government. He gave me your name."

Jordan smiled.

Amy told her story.

Mrs. Cedillo's husband was shot one night after sundown. He had been standing near an open window in their high rise apartment. They were enjoying a pleasant conversation while she sat at the dining room table reviewing paperwork from the office. He had been looking outside, admiring the city lights, and then turned back to face her. A red dot appeared on his shirt and a small puff of dust clung to a nearby wall.

"It had to be murder. He was right by the window. Who just randomly shoots someone standing near a window that is so high up?"

"You'd be surprised. But I'll look into this, using every connection I have. I will find your husband's killer if humanly possible."

Amy Cedillo left a five figure check on Jordan's desk and walked out.

Jordan stared at the check for a moment, gave the woman five minutes to leave the area, and then closed the offices.

She could accomplish more from home.

"Hmmm, let's start with cell phone numbers used."

Jordan entered the search parameters into the web site, using the victim's zip code and those adjacent to where the victim had died.

"Next, we limit the search to 2 months prior and two months following the homicide."

121

The data flooded the screen, pages and pages of it.

"Wow. Just in that one part of L.A."

Next, she refined the search so phone numbers were displayed for phones that had remained in the area for one hour or more.

She repeated the last search and piped the data into a file.

"Now we search for names in the file and match those names associated with people deceased or missing."

One name came up. Steve Underwood.

"Hello, Mr. Underwood."

Click click click.

"Hmmm … you didn't live around there, but you were hanging around there a lot.

"Let's take a look at your spending habits, Mr. Underwood."

She retrieved his credit and debit card information and created a file with the information containing the data.

"Now we do a dump of all the residents renting or owning in the area during the four months."

She wrote a program to read the residents' names and download their spending habits to see if they were shopping in stores while Mr. Underwood was paying for a purchase, indicating friends or significant others who might have been shopping with him.

"Maybe we'll get a match, Imaginary J.T."

She petted the stuffed tiger sitting near the keyboard and walked away while the program ran.

"David Niven. Like the old actor."

She went to a Federal firearms website.

"Let's see if you own any guns.

"Wow. You like your guns, Mr. Niven."

One particular firearm's caliber caught her eye. It was the same caliber weapon used to kill her client's husband.

Jordan cocked her head to one side and smiled up at the apartment door's peephole.

The man on the other side of the door saw a woman wearing cheap drug store leopard print sunglasses dressed in black and white housekeeper's attire, her hands enclosed in yellow cleaning gloves. The bucket, mop, plastic cleaning supplies caddy, and vacuum cleaner strengthened the housekeeper image.

"Acme Housekeeping," said Jordan, knocking on the door again.

The man opened the door a few inches.

"I don't have a maid service."

"It's a free service, sir. A free trial. Your apartment complex paid for it."

"It's dark outside. Why the sunglasses?"

"Safety issues. The company asks us to provide our own eye protection."

"And the cleaning doesn't cost a thing?"

Jordan smiled as he opened the door a bit wider.

"That's correct.

"I don't need your email, phone number or other formal ID, but I do need to confirm your name.

"Is it David Niven?"

"Yes."

"Like the actor?"

"Just like the actor.   Only I'm alive."

She smiled again.

"Yes, I can see that. May I come in and clean your apartment, Mr. Niven?"

"Yes, you may."

"Thank you."

"Let me help you with your stuff."

"Thanks!" said Jordan.

"The elevator helps, but it's still brutal lugging this stuff around," she said.

She looked around the apartment as Mr. Niven brought the vacuum cleaner, mop, and bucket inside the apartment.

She began dusting immediately. Niven moved to the kitchen area.

"You don't mind me dusting do you?"

"No. I'll just stand over here."

"Great. Some people have allergies, so I always ask."

She moved around the living area and could see into the dining area.

"Wow, you have a lot of guns on your table."

"Not that many."

"Well, you have more than three looks like. It's not a big deal. It's just an observation. I have an uncle that's into guns.

"So do you live alone?"

"Yes. Why do you ask?"

"It affects my company's bottom line. More people, more dirt."

"I never thought about it that way."

"I clean a lot of places. It makes sense."

"You don't say?"

"Yep. Look through the window. You see that high rise apartment building half a mile away? I clean that building, too."

"Really?"

Jordan went back to her dusting.

"Yep. A couple of months ago, one of my clients got shot. He was just standing there at his window. You can see the apartment's window through your window. If you had your window open at the time, you might have even heard the shot."

Niven stared at her.

"His wife thinks it was murder.

"They haven't caught anyone yet though. It's a good thing you have all these guns. Nobody will mess with you.

"But I guess stuff happens everywhere in the city. Anybody ever been shot around here?"

He stared at her a moment before speaking.

"Not that I know of. We had a suicide a couple of years ago. Kinda messy."

"Yeah, I hate that kind of cleanup.

"I did hear about one guy that disappeared around here."

"What guy?" David asked.

"Steve something. A friend who cleans another building near this one told me about it. I think this complex is run by the same company."

Niven glanced at his guns for a moment. Jordan noticed.

"Yeah, Steve Whatever disappeared after visiting this building."

"How do they know that?"

"Cell phone records and such I guess. The government does that kind of stuff.

"Steve Underwood. That was his name.

"You wouldn't know anything about that would you, Mr. Niven? Did you know him?"

"No."

"I mean with all those guns … accidents can happen."

"An accident could happen right now."

"Hey, I'm not a cop. I was just saying. You got a lot of guns here. Steve Underwood had a lot of guns.

"And the man in the other building, he was shot with a gun the same caliber as that one on your table.

"Did you know that no one else in this building owns a gun except you? Only you, David."

"Who are you?"

"Somebody who doesn't like seeing good people get hurt.

"What was it, David? You two get into an argument?"

Jordan backed away as Niven moved toward the kitchen table.

"I'm going to ask you again, Miss Cleaning Lady. Who are you? Are you FBI?"

"No."

"Some other kind of Fed?"

"No."

"What are you doing here? Are you some kind of nosey spy?"

"Well ..."

She looked into a nearby open pantry. Inside, she could see a child's red sneaker.

Like His red sneaker.

Like the ones that sat inside His old closet near His old bed. The twin bed she slept in most nights.

She leaned forward to take a better look at the pantry's contents.

It was her involuntary curiosity that moved her head out of the oncoming bullet's path.

She snapped back to reality and reached into a skirt pocket.

Her hand came out with a small .22 caliber pistol which she used to shoot David Niven in the bottom of his skull. The bullet exited through the top of his head.

Before his head hit the floor, she was moving toward a similar .22 caliber pistol on his kitchen table.

She switched out the cylinders in the guns and placed his own gun next to his body.

She put a written confession to the two deaths on the kitchen table.

She walked over to the pantry to look at the shoe.

She took a moment. She allowed herself to think back, to remember, to feel a happier time.

Before the Younger He died.

Before the Older He gave up and left.

When she had so many dreams and didn't know how easily they could end.

When she had her original middle name and not her dead son's.

She sighed.   All the air and all the life went out of her for a few moments.

She straightened up and moved her vacuum cleaner and cleaning supplies into a hallway closet.

Opening the vacuum's collection canister, she removed a length of climbing rope and a collapsible grappling hook.

She then reconnected the canister and shut the closet door.

Walking outside to the apartment's small balcony, she closed the sliding door behind her. She checked the alley/walkway below for passersby and, seeing none, she attached the climbing rope to the railing and flung herself over the handrail, slowing her descent with her rubber cleaning gloves.

When she reached the ground she jiggled and tugged on the rope a few times until the grappling hook disconnected from the railing above and fell to the ground. She detached the metal device and threw it in a nearby dumpster and discarded the rope behind the dumpster.

She walked to the front of David Niven's apartment building and paused at the sidewalk. It was dark out and the streetlights showed only a few people walking by, satisfied with life in their own worlds.

She remembered other nights, walking alone after an evening's tasks were done.

Tonight she didn't have to be alone.

She took out her cell phone. It was three blocks to the minivan. She had plenty of time to choose between Jackie and Tonya.

Weighing her options, she smiled.

In the shadows, half a block behind her, The Phantom stepped out from the shadows.

The Phantom had seen her go inside the building with cleaning equipment and noticed her descent from the balcony. Now The Phantom watched her disappear from view.

"Who is this woman?"

THE END

POSTSCRIPT

Such is Life in Jordan's World.

Such is the Path of Jordan St. Clair.

Bob Tillman, JSC-HQ

APPENDIX A

This book is intended to entertain and to serve as the basis for a television show (or shows) or possibly a motion picture. The original casting suggestions at the time of its writing are as follows:

Jackie Faraday: Katee Sackhoff

Tonya Manning: Riki Lindhome

Jordan St. Clair: Kate Micucci

APPENDIX B

The suggested theme song for the television show *insanity* is the Woody Woodpecker theme song.

The suggested theme song for the television show *Jordan's World* is the Peter Gunn theme song.

The Elvis song Jordan sings is "The Wonder of You".

APPENDIX C

There are many layers to *insanity*. One of the intended purposes is to promote new television shows before the regular season starts and to increase viewership during the Holiday Season. For its core cast members, its original purpose is to serve as a lucrative part-time job to allow for their busy schedules.

APPENDIX D

With regard to merchandising, I suggest a scale model of the Project Support minivan. Each core cast member and celebrity guest star will have action figures created to ride inside the miniature version of the minivan.

www.ingramcontent.com/pod-product-compliance
Lightning Source LLC
Chambersburg PA
CBHW060618130626
46555CB00002B/564